THE GOLD HUNTERS

THE GOLD HUNTERS

by

Alan C. Porter

Dales Large Print Books
Long Preston, North Yorkshire,
BD23 4ND, England.

British Library Cataloguing in Publication Data.

Porter, Alan C.
The gold hunters.

A catalogue record of this book is available from the British Library

ISBN 978-1-84262-563-7 pbk

First published in Great Britain in 1992 by Robert Hale Limited

Published in Large Print 2007 by arrangement with Robert Hale Ltd.

Dales Large Print is an imprint of Library Magna Books Ltd.

Printed and bound in Great Britain by
T.J. (International) Ltd., Cornwall, PL28 8RW

To Mum and Dad

ONE

The conestoga moved through the night hauled by a team of six. A light wind caused the canvas to billow and slap about its curved, wooden ribs. Shadows, silent and ghost-like flitted over the land as wind driven clouds raced across the mottled face of the moon. Stones crunched beneath the metal rimmed wheels and kicked from beneath the shod hooves of the snorting team. The wagon was purpose built from an extra set of wheels to spread the load. The tracks left by its six wheels cut deep into the trail. It was built to carry weight and now it was fully loaded.

The wagon moved slowly, stealthily through the night. With it rode ten, silent riders in cavalry uniform, leather creaking and metal buckles jangling on harness. They rode between a series of low hills patched with black, moving shadows. Inside the special wagon lay three tiers of wooden boxes, containing within their wooden walls a million dollars of gold bullion.

The men knew of the wealth therein, but Major Phillips, riding level with the driver and his mate, knew something else. He felt his stomach tighten as the trail dipped toward a stand of trees. He knew that in a few short minutes everyone riding with the wagon would be dead, their fate sealed long before they entered the trees. Beneath the cover of his cape Major Phillips drew his Navy Colt and waited in anticipation.

The keen eye of the driver picked out the fallen tree blocking the trail as for a few moments the moon found open space to sail in. Its silver beams broke through the trees in a series of misty bars and lit the trail ahead with broken light. He hauled back on the reins cursing.

'Trail's blocked ahead, Major,' he growled.

'Smith, Davis, Calloway, Grant. Get forward and move the tree,' Major Phillips barked, glad that the night hid the sheen of sweat that had broken out over his face.

The four men rode forward and dismounted and these were the first to die as the night erupted into a series of gunshots and flashes from the trees. Phillips, mouth dry, heart hammering in his chest, flipped his cape aside and fired point blank at the driver and his mate. The driver was thrown back into the wagon while his mate toppled over the far side of the wagon. The remainder of the troop, five men, were cut down from the sides. In a few short moments the deadly ambush was over with only Major Phillips left alive.

Figures stirred from the trees, weapons smoking in their gloved hands. Four figures clad in long, black duster coats and black pointed hoods which hid their faces.

'We did it,' Phillips sang out, voice dry and croaky. 'A million dollars in gold. At last I'll be able to dump this damn uniform and live in style.' He grinned nervously and ran a hand across his dry lips.

'Indeed we did,' a voice agreed, muffled by the confines of the hood that he had made no attempt to remove. The speaker stepped forward. 'Unfortunately, Major, a decision has been reached that concerns you. We feel that you could be a liability to our continued freedom.'

'I don't understand?' Major Phillips' voice wavered. 'We had a deal...'

'Look at it from our point of view.' The speaker cut in smoothly. 'A major escorting a gold shipment that gets stolen, suddenly retiring with a large fortune would be a little too coincidental for the authorities to ignore.'

A cold feeling washed through Phillips.

'What the hell are you saying? I fixed this whole thing up. Without me none of this would have happened.'

'True, Major, but also true is the fact that without you we can be sure it will continue to happen to our benefit.' The Winchester in the speaker's hands flashed fire. As the single detonation fled through the trees the bullet caught the major on the bridge of the nose and blew the back of his head away as it exited. The major's horse whinnied in alarm and side-stepped nervously as its rider pitched from the saddle and thudded to the ground. In a well-organized display of planning, two men used horses to drag the obstruction from the trail while the others bundled the dead soldiers into the wagon and collected up their mounts. A leafy branch was used to scrub out the blood-stains and fifteen minutes after entering the trees the wagon emerged and disappeared into the night.

'I'm willing to pay the going rate plus an extra dollar a day and all found for any man willing to toss his bedroll into the Boxed P spread.' The speaker was a tall, slim, red-haired woman in her early twenties clad in levis and a tan, buckskin jacket. The latter lay open to reveal a red check shirt beneath. The mannish clothes did little to hide the womanly figure. Her green eyes flashed anxiously at the group of men who had gathered on Freedom's dusty main street. She stood on the creaking boards of the sidewalk before Clancey's saloon.

Eyes in the group flickered nervously to the three men who lounged by the saloon batwings a few yards to the right of the redhead. Then muttering and shaking their heads the group began to break up and disperse.

'You're wasting your time, Miss Parsons. Ain't gonna get no takers for that bit o' chicken scratching you call a spread.' A wagon rumbled by springs groaning and leather creaking. The words came from one of the three loungers. A big-bellied man in leather chaps and scuffed, dirty boots. Stubble darkened his heavy face. He grinned as he spoke and his companions grinned with him. With thumbs hooked on his gunbelt the man moved a few paces forward. 'Best sell out to the Circle C while you can.'

Angela Parsons rounded angrily on the man, eyes flashing green fire. Today was her last attempt to find hands to help her run the Boxed P. Without them she was beaten. It was not that Freedom lacked the men, only that the men lacked the backbone to go against Milt Clayburn's Circle C riders like the ones she faced now: hard, vicious men with little regard for the health and safety of others. Beaten she might have been, but she refused to show it.

'Tell your boss that the Boxed P is not for sale,' she snapped at him.

'He ain't gonna like that,' the speaker pointed out in a leisurely fashion.

'My heart bleeds,' she scoffed biting back the tears of frustration that threatened to spill from her eyes.

'The range is no place for a woman.' He jerked a thumb over his shoulder. 'In there's where you belong. On your back earning a dollar or two,' he said spitefully, and his companions laughed coarsely. Angela's face reddened. Her fists balled at her sides. She would dearly have loved to have struck the unlovely, fleshy face that leered down at her, but she had no reservations about the owner of the face, Billy Redland. Given the provocation he would hit back regardless, caring not whether his opponent was man, woman or child.

'Ma'am.' A voice turned her head. A boy, no more than sixteen limped forward a battered hat clasped in thin hands. He had remained as the others dispersed. Red suspenders crossing over narrow shoulders held a pair of frayed, black pants in place. He wore heavy, black lace-up boots and topped the whole ensemble off with a grubby yellow shirt. 'Name's Willy Tate. I gotta busted leg, but I can ride and build fences and tend horses real good.' He gave Billy Redland a defiant glance as he spoke.

Angela's anger softened as she looked into the hopeful, upturned face topped with a tangle of straw-coloured hair.

'Haven't I seen you working in the livery?'

'Yes, ma'am, but I'm looking to better

myself if you'll have me.'

A bray of coarse laughter from Billy Redland made the boy wince.

'What about your folks, Willy?' Angela ignored Billy Redland.

'Ain't got none, ma'am. Not as I can recall.'

'What about Mr Billings at the livery?'

'He done fired me this morning, ma'am.' Willy hung his head. 'Said I was no good for anything.' He raised his head again, hopelessness replacing the earlier hope. 'Guess I ain't what you're looking for.' He jammed the hat on to his head. 'Sorry to have troubled you, ma'am.' He turned away.

'Wait!' Angela called. 'You build fences you say?'

'Real strong,' Willy boasted back.

'You're hired, Willy,' Angela replied and a smile lit up the boy's face. 'Collect your things and meet me by the green wagon outside the general store.'

'Got nothing to collect, ma'am,' Willy said shamefacedly.

'Then we'll get you something.'

'Sure is something.' Billy Redland wiped tears of laughter from his eyes. 'You came to town for a ranch crew and ended up with one gimpy kid. Wait until I tell Mr Clayburn.'

'Make that three, ma'am. You can add us to the payroll,' a new voice broke in.

All eyes turned to the owner of the voice and his companion. The speaker stood an inch or two under the six foot mark with dark hair curling about his ears from beneath the brim of a short crowned stetson. He had a pleasant, smiling face dominated by a pair of piercing, blue eyes. The blue levis and chestnut brown, hide jacket that covered his powerful frame were well worn, but clean. Boots, coat and hat all matched in colour while a yellow shirt peeped from the open front of the jacket. But it was his companion who caught the attention.

At six foot six he commanded a respectful stare and Angela swallowed as her eyes took in his imposing form clad from head to foot in light tan buckskin, tan boots and hat. The only splash of colour came from a red bandanna at his throat. Apart from his huge, wide-shouldered frame, his most startling attribute lay in a mane of silver hair that flowed about his head, revealed because his hat rested on his shoulders, its cord about his throat. The hair caught and held her attention. It was neither white or grey, but a wonderful silver. The eyebrows were the same colour. Even the eyes were slate grey chips in the tanned face.

A smile twitched the tall man's lips and Angela looked away feeling a hot flush burn itself into her cheeks. Both men wore gunbelts, holsters tied down. The smaller man favoured a single action, Army Colt, the Peacemaker, while his companion an older, double-action Adams, a British-made gun used extensively on both sides during the Civil War. In addition he carried a broad-bladed bowie knife in an ornate, Indian-crafted sheath on his other hip.

'I haven't seen you about town before,' she

stammered, returning her gaze to the smaller of the two.

'No, ma'am. We're new and looking for work. Wes Hardiman at your service.' Wes smiled disarmingly.

'And Ben Travis,' the silver-haired giant added. 'You made an offer we couldn't refuse.' His smile was equally as disarming. Both men were in their early/mid twenties and that made the silver-haired man even more remarkable in her opinion.

'You know ranch work?' she asked. 'And cattle?'

'Sure do, ma'am,' Wes replied. 'Trail-bossed a few herds west in my time and Ben here was brought up on a ranch.'

'Then you're hired,' she said quickly. 'Meet me at the green wagon by the general store in thirty minutes and we'll go out to the ranch.'

'Yes, ma'am,' Wes tipped his hat.

'Come on, Willy, you can help me ... Willy!' The boy, mesmerized at the size of Ben, jumped and limped in her wake, casting awed glances back over his shoulder at Ben.

'Reckon a beer'll wash the trail dust away while we wait,' Wes said and a smile spread across Ben's face.

'How about a barrel? It's been a long ride.'

The two entered the saloon with hardly a glance at the three, now scowling, loungers.

'Are you gonna drink that or die of thirst staring at it?' Wes asked a few moments later when drinks bought they had retired to a centre table. The saloon was about half full and their entrance had drawn a more than usual covert stare. It was aimed mainly at Ben, but if the big man noticed he paid no attention as he stared raptly at the foaming mug before him.

'Just appreciating the moment,' Ben replied with a grin. At that moment a shadow fell across the two. It was Billy Redland and his two companions.

''Day gents,' he greeted as Wes and Ben looked up. 'You're strangers in town.'

A quirky smile touched Wes's lips.

'Pure fact I can't deny,' Wes admitted.

'First thing strangers learn is that they don't tie into the Boxed P. It ain't healthy.' Billy gave a grin that wavered as two unsmiling faces looked back at him.

'Is that a fact?' Wes mused. 'And who might you be, Mister?'

'Billy Redland. Me and the boys,' he waved a hand at the silent pair. 'Ride for the Circle C and if'n you've got any sense that's where you should be headed.'

'Never did have much sense,' Wes admitted almost regretfully.

'It's the only outfit in these parts to ride for,' Billy pressed, not liking the cool, calm front the man was displaying.

'Seems like you're wrong, Mister. Ben and me are signed to the Boxed P.'

'Maybe you still got trail dust in your ears, friend,' Billy grated ominously. 'You either work for the Circle C or you don't work here at all.' He glared down at Wes.

'Now why might that be?' Ben drawled taking over from Wes.

'Cause that's the way it is, friend. Milt Clayburn is the top man around Freedom. You either ride with him or agin him and I don't recommend the agin.'

'Said Milt Clayburn being the owner of this Circle C spread,' Ben said.

'You'd better believe it,' Billy growled. 'I'm allowing that you're strangers and don't know no better, but now I've acquainted you with the facts it makes horse sense you do the right thing.'

'There you go again using that word sense.' Wes shook his head regretfully. 'Let's see, Mister Redland. A dollar says that I've got more sense than you.' He eyed the heavy face quizzically.

'I ain't with you, friend,' Billy said after flashing his two companions a puzzled glance.

'Reckon I'll have to show you,' Wes said rising to his feet and fishing a dollar from his pocket. Ben rolled his eyes as if to say, 'here we go again' and reluctantly took his concentration off the mug before him.

'Keep an eye on the dollar, boy,' Wes said and flipped the coin towards the high ceiling of the saloon. Three heads craned to watch its progress. In fact most heads in the saloon watched the spinning coin, so most of them missed the punch that Wes unloaded on the point of Billy's jaw. Taken completely by surprise the man flew backwards, landed flat on his back on a table that tipped over and pitched him unceremoniously across two chairs. Even as his body scattered the chairs, snapping the legs from one, Wes deftly reached out and caught the returning coin. Those in the saloon stared on in stunned surprise.

'One of these days...' Ben admonished.

'Not met the man yet with a lick of sense to keep his eye off the coin,' Wes replied with a grin dancing in his blue eyes. At that moment the nearer of Billy Redland's two cronies, a stocky, beef-shouldered individual, gave a roar and threw himself at Wes, fists folded into granite-like hammers ready to pulverize the dark-haired man.

Wes met the charge, deflecting the blow and pushing it aside with his left arm whilst jabbing at the man's mid-section with his right. 'Smiley' Jones folded over, air whistling from his puckered lips only seeing at the last second the knee that was rising to meet his descending face. Smiley sailed backwards, hitting the floor and sliding into an empty table.

The last of the three, rake-handle thin, face gaunt and skull-like beneath a black hat with a band of silver conchos decorating the crown, was already in the process of pulling his gun. Half the barrel was still in its holster when he found himself staring pop-eyed down the barrel of a Colt Peacemaker. The speed of Wes's draw brought gasps from the onlookers followed by a silence that was intense.

'Make your choice, cowboy. Live or die?' Wes breathed softly, eyes ice hard in a now grim, taut face.

Joe Santos made the choice by letting his gun drop back into its holster and lifting his hands clear. His movements made the conchos on his hat tinkle.

'You've made a big mistake, fella. When Red comes around he ain't gonna be too happy.' If those words were supposed to have a sobering effect on Wes they merely solicited a thin, bored smile.

'I'll bear it in mind,' Wes replied as a groaning Smiley Jones came unsteadily to his feet holding a grubby blue bandanna to a bleeding nose. 'I suggest you take yourselves and good old Billy out of here. You make the place look untidy.' Wes reholstered his gun. The two, the fight gone out of them for the moment, did as Wes said, hauling Billy out between them.

'You sure have a way of making friends,' Ben observed dryly as Wes resumed his seat.

'Must be my natural charm,' Wes replied with a lopsided grin, then he scowled at his friend. 'I didn't see you helping.'

'You didn't appear to be needing any. 'Sides, me and my friend here were getting acquainted.' He indicated the now empty mug. 'Brawling sure is a thirsty business.'

Wes was about to make a suitable remark when a cackling old-timer with white, tobacco-stained whiskers appeared before the two, the saloon coming back to life around them.

'That was sure somethin', Mister,' he praised, black, button eyes alive with amusement above a gap-toothed grin. 'Name's Stumpy.'

'Wes, and this here's, Ben.' Wes exchanged amused looks with Ben. 'If'n you figure on taking up where Billy left off, then I'm out of here.' He eyed the old Dragoon pistol in a holster that had swivelled to hang between the oldster's legs.

This amused Stumpy and he set to cackling away in his beard making both men laugh.

'Hell no, boys,' Stumpy finally spluttered. 'Say, you really signed up with Miss Angie?'

'If you mean the red-headed lady you heard right,' Wes agreed.

'Then we'll be seeing a piece of each

other. I drive the wagon for her and help out where I can and it don't do to keep her waiting. She's gotta mean tongue if'n she wants to use it.'

'Then lead on, Stumpy,' Wes said with a grin after downing his beer and climbing to his feet. Ben followed reluctantly, he could have used a refill.

Billy Redland and his companions were outside when the two, headed by Stumpy, left Clancey's. Billy's eyes were still glassy as he sat in a chair.

'We'll meet again, Mister,' he growled at Wes.

'That's your funeral,' Wes retorted as he walked away.

'There you go again,' Ben complained as the two collected their horses, a big black for Ben and an attractive paint for Wes, and walked towards the wagon, 'upsetting the local citizens.' But he was smiling as he spoke.

Angela was sitting on the seat of the flat-bed as the three arrived while Willy found a space amid the supplies to squat in the rear. She looked up as Stumpy hauled himself into the driving-seat, her green eyes falling on the two.

'Didn't know if you had changed your mind,' she called.

'Well,' Wes swung astride his paint, 'someone had a go at changing it, but they didn't have a strong enough argument.'

At the reins Stumpy guffawed and in a few quick sentences relayed to her the incident in the saloon. Afterwards she gazed a little angrily at Wes.

'I'm sorry you found it necessary to do that, Mr Hardiman. There is enough antagonism between the Circle C and Boxed P as it is. This will only serve to increase it.' Then a smile touched her lips and filled her eyes. 'All the same I wish I could have been there to see it. Move out, Stumpy.'

TWO

The ride from Freedom took them north across a vast, undulating plain of lush grass towards the high, broken ridge of the Wyoming Rockies; a grey, forbidding rampart of grey rising through a mantle of green pine to the blue, summer sky above. Very little was said until an hour out of town Angela had Stumpy halt the wagon at the top of a rise. There was pride in her eyes as she turned a smiling face to Wes and Ben who had ridden alongside.

'There it is, gentlemen, the Boxed P.' She waved a hand ahead.

Below them lay a broad, lush valley that merged into the folds and ripples of the foothills at the base of the mountains. Before the foothills, close to where a stream broke clear of the hills and gullies and meandered its way out into the valley, lay a collection of buildings against a blackcloth of trees. A white fence circled the buildings and within that a corral attached to a big barn. Against the backdrop of the mountains and good cattle country spreading away in all directions, the ranch was ideally situated.

'Mighty purty, ma'am,' Wes acknowledged, his keen eyes noting the tiny herds of cattle scattered to all horizons. 'Whereat's the Circle C?'

'Ten miles to the west. You can't see it from here.'

'How many head of cattle do you run, ma'am?' Ben asked.

'Fifteen hundred at the last tally.'

'Sizeable herd,' Ben replied. 'Need a bit of rounding up.'

'I need to get them to market, Mr Travis, if I'm to keep this place.'

'Call me, Ben, ma'am. It's a mite less wearisome on the tongue,' Ben invited.

'When you're through socializing,' Wes interrupted with a grin, 'why are the Circle

C boys so fired up to get your property? By the way I answer best to Wes. It's even less wearisome than Ben.' He flashed a quick look at Ben who refused to be drawn.

Angela smiled at the gentle rivalry between the two friends before growing serious again at the question.

'I don't know, Wes. My grandfather ran the Boxed P alongside Milt Clayburn's Circle C for years. Six months ago grandfather died in a riding accident and left the Boxed P to me. Clayburn offered to buy me out, but I guess I fell in love with the place. I was born and raised in Chicago. I never met grandfather more than once when he came to Chicago on business. My mama died some five years back and Chicago's not the best place to live alone. When I learned of my inheritance I was off like a shot, glad to get away. I liked what I saw and figured to get a few hands together and run the ranch.'

'Tough business for a woman,' Ben said.

'Women can do other things than work in saloons,' she flared back and was instantly sorry at her show of temper. 'Sorry, Ben. It comes from a lifetime of being told what I can do and what I can't do.'

'Ain't nothing to be sorry for, ma'am,' Ben said. 'Go on with your story.'

'When I wouldn't sell, Milt Clayburn stopped being friendly. The hands I had hired suddenly began leaving and wouldn't say why. I tried to hire more and that's when I found out that it was Clayburn's hired guns who were frightening them off. I tried hiring from outside but after a few weeks the men packed in, scared off, and that's how it's been. They didn't worry when Stumpy hired on and you saw what happened when Willy here offered his services. It's a continuous pressure to force me to sell up and I don't know why. From what I learned from people in town, Milt Clayburn and my grandfather were good friends up until he died. I thought I would get support from Clayburn, help if I needed it, but he's doing his best to drive me out.' She shrugged helplessly.

'You ever faced this Clayburn to find out what he's up to?' Wes asked.

'Oh yes. He just said I would ruin the land. It would be better if I sold to him and bought a dress shop back east.' Colour burnt in her cheeks at the thought and her fists clenched. 'I told him what he could do with his idea.'

'I'd have liked to have been there at the time, ma'am,' Wes replied with a grin at Ben.

The spirit faded from the girl's eyes and she looked pleadingly at Wes and Ben.

'I haven't much left to fight him with. Unless I can get the cattle to market in Laramie, Milt Clayburn will get his wish. Grandfather had a sizeable bank loan and selling the cattle is the only way I have of repaying it.'

'Don't worry, ma'am, we'll get your cattle to market,' Ben drawled with quiet confidence.

'You can do that?' She sounded doubtful and it was Stumpy who provided the answer.

'I get the feel that them boys can do just what they please. We gotta couple of live ones here, Miss Angie.'

Angie smiled wanly. She wasn't too sure she believed in miracles, but just in case...

'Best we get to the ranch. Martha gets a mite touchy if she's left on her own for too long. Move on, Stumpy.'

Twenty minutes later the group rode between the high gateposts beneath a cracked wooden sign that bore, in fading yellow, a P inside a yellow square. Close up the signs of neglect that distance had softened became all too apparent. Parts of the outer fence had collapsed and other parts leaned at drunken angles.

The long, low bunkhouse, as they passed, showed a number of windows boarded over where broken glass had never been replaced. The two big barns beyond the bunkhouse and set a little back from it, displayed weather-sprung boards. The one nearest the end of the bunkhouse had lost its big double doors as the frame had rotted.

These now were canted at an angle against the wooden wall. The remains of a flatbed wagon lay before the barn. Wheels gone, it lay ignored and forgotten as weeds and grass grew through its rotting body. A rusting plough gave mute evidence that once someone had tried to till the land before giving it over to cattle.

At the end of the furthest barn a small corral jutted at right angles across their path and to the left of that lay the ranch house itself: a low, single-storey structure made from pine logs that had been hauled from the lower slopes of the mountains. A fine stone chimney dominated the end of the house they approached. Of all the buildings this was the only one that looked to be in good shape. The sloping overhang of the roof timbers were supported on good, strong beams, and white-painted shutters fastened back beside curtained windows. The creek, emerging from a thin stand of oak, flowed behind the barns and a second stand of oak stood at the far corner of the house.

As they veered to the left, past the corral to the house, Wes noted a half completed building beyond the corral. It boasted four walls of crude, clay bricks breached by an opening for a door and two frameless windows. It still waited for a roof, the wooden spars in place to support it giving Wes the uncomfortable impression of a half rotted animal carcass. It was clothed in patchy weed and vine.

'As you can see the place needs some attention,' Angela said apologetically as Stumpy brought the wagon to a halt before the house.

'I've seen worse,' Ben replied mildly as he swung down from the saddle.

'Are you always this tactful, Ben?' She raised an enquiring eyebrow. 'It's in a terrible state.'

'Yes, ma'am,' Ben replied with a grin as the front door opened and a fat negress, head crowned with a mop of frizzy, grey hair appeared wiping her hands on a pink, gingham apron she wore. Her eyes popped at the sight of Ben.

'Lordy, Miss Angie. That boy's gonna need some feeding. It's got a long ways to go down.'

Angela laughed and introduced the three newcomers, ending up with, 'And this is Martha, a real treasure.'

Martha giggled and let her gaze drop on Willy, head shaking.

'Boy, there's more meat on mah broom handle than what's on you. Well we'll soon put a bit of flesh on them bones or mah name's not Martha. I reckon you'all could do with a bite of something now. Is that all right, Miss Angie?'

'Sure, Martha.'

'Got some real fine cornbread, baked fresh today and there's cold beef for the cutting. I reckon that should hold you till supper.' She headed back into the house to get the food ready followed by Angie while Wes, Ben and Willy helped Stumpy unload the wagon. Afterwards Wes and Ben unsaddled their horses and turned them into the corral before going in search of the promised food.

Ten miles away at the Circle C a less than friendly meeting was in progress. Milt Clayburn listened with growing anger as Billy Redland, flanked by Smiley and Joe, told his story. Clayburn sat behind a big, leather-topped mahogany desk. The wall at his back lay hidden behind a covering of books. Not that Clayburn had much use for books, but they looked good. The other three walls were display cases for Clayburn's hunting prowess. Deer, wolf, bear, bison, cougar and others decorated the cool, white walls. The polished, wooden blocks of the floor were scattered with colourful Indian rugs. Sunlight glancing through elegant french windows to his left fell across the front edge of the desk and drew pictures on the opposite wall.

'And you did nothing?' he stormed at the humiliated Redland.

'He suckered us, boss. Tricked me into watching this damn coin and hit me when I wasn't looking. Must have hit my head as I went down. Smiley here he got with a lucky punch and somehow he managed to get the drop on Joe.'

'There was two of 'em,' Smiley threw in. 'The other was built like the side of a mountain.' It was a statement all the men agreed on with vigorous nods of the head that less than impressed Clayburn.

'But you said he did nothing,' Clayburn pointed out icily. 'It was the smaller one that made fools out of you.' He rose to his feet a sneer on his handsome, bearded face.

Milt Clayburn was a tall man in his mid forties without an ounce of excess flesh on his lean, rugged frame. His only concession to age was a dusting of grey at the temples of his dark, curly hair that matched the curls of his beard. He was clad in a tailored dark-blue three piece suit. The gold chain of a timepiece hung across his lower vest. His light blue shirt was of the finest cotton with a black, bootlace tie at his throat. There was a swarthiness about his features that suggested Indian or Mexican blood somewhere in the past.

'But he might have done,' Smiley pointed out. 'We'uns had to keep an eye on him and that's how the other fella got the drop on us.' His speech brought approving nods from the other two.

Clayburn's face darkened. He moved around to the front of the desk before them and hitched a single buttock on the edge of the desk, thumbs hooked into the lower pockets of his vest.

'Enough of these feeble excuses,' he barked. 'Because of your stupidity the whole town is now aware of what happened at the saloon and it might encourage others to sign up for the Boxed P and that would never do. What did you say these strangers were called?'

'The smaller of the two was Wes Hardiman. The big boy Ben Travis,' Joe Santos supplied.

Clayburn shook his head. The names meant nothing to him.

'Good. Now get out of here and find out all you can about the two. From what you say they don't sound like ordinary cowhands.'

'They tote their guns real low and tied down,' Smiley said.

'All the more reason to find out who they are and why they are here. Until we know more you keep away from them. You three get into town and start asking around. Get a wire off to McCloud in Laramie with their names and descriptions. Try the sheriff's pile of wanted posters. Just get me something and don't come back until you have.'

Clayburn stood there, deep in thought, some minutes after they had left. He had been too soft on her. Now was the time to step up the campaign to get her out, but first a visit was called for.

'Rider coming in,' Wes sang out.

It was late afternoon with the sun throwing long shadows from the trees and buildings. With Ben and Willy the three had settled for getting the fence fixed. In the first barn they found poles, posts and nails galore and so they had set to with some gusto. Wes and Ben had shucked their shirts and wore tatty work pants. Their upper bodies were sheened in sweat.

'It's Milt Clayburn,' Willy announced.

Wes smiled mirthlessly.

'Ain't that just something? Willy get the gate closed.'

'On his own too,' Ben observed as both men pulled on old shirts and waited.

'Milt Clayburn to see Miss Angela Parsons,' Clayburn called as he reined his mount to a halt before the gate.

Wes eyed him over the gate.

'Willy. Go tell Miss Angie that she has a visitor,' he called, eyes remaining on the mounted man.

A smile touched Clayburn's lips and then was gone.

'Heard that a couple of strangers had hired out to the Boxed P,' he said. He noted the tied down holsters the two wore even as they repaired fences and saw no reason to change his earlier opinion. These two were no ordinary cowboys.

'You heard right,' Wes replied coolly.

'You'd get a better deal at the Circle C,' Clayburn said mildly. 'The Boxed P is dead. It just don't know when to lie down.'

'You're entitled to your opinion, Mister,' Wes replied without rancour. The two were testing each other. Prodding, poking to get reaction, using words to build a picture of the other's strengths and weaknesses. So far Ben had not joined in. The silver-haired giant had remained silent. Wes, he had sized up, as being cool and dangerous, but the other was an unknown quantity.

'Don't your friend have anything to say?' Clayburn asked and Wes grinned sardonically.

'Ben here's choosy about whom he parleys with. Me...' He shrugged. 'I guess I haven't got any taste.'

Clayburn stiffened in the saddle and for a second anger darkened his face, but he forced himself to remain calm. Wes noted that his jibe struck home and smiled.

'You may learn to regret those words,' Clayburn retorted through a fixed smile that never reached his eyes. Wes never got a chance to reply. At that moment Angela Parsons arrived with Willy and Stumpy in tow.

'What do you want, Mr Clayburn?' Angela asked frostily.

'Just dropped by to see if you've considered my offer,' Clayburn said casually.

'I thought I'd made myself clear on that point. The Boxed P is not for sale. To you or anyone,' Angela replied stiffly.

'Have it your way, Miss Parsons. The Boxed P will end up as mine no matter what.' He spoke confidently, smiled all the time.

Angela's cheeks flushed with anger.

'Get off my land, Clayburn. You're not welcome here.'

'As you will, Miss Parsons, but I hope to be saying those very same words to you in the near future.' His gaze fell on Wes. 'You and your friend will be out of a job soon, so enjoy it while you can. By the way, you're making a good job of *my* fence.' He swung the horse's head and dug his heels into its flanks, laughing as he rode away.

'Confident sort of fella isn't he,' Wes remarked.

'That man!' Angela cried stamping her foot in frustration.

'Don't go getting yourself upset over the likes of him, ma'am. He talks a lot and mostly hot air,' Wes said.

She sagged limply.

'Maybe not, Wes. He holds all the cards and I'm just being pig-headed. To keep this place I need to get my cattle to market and without men that would take a miracle.' A glint of tears sparkled in her green eyes.

'Well I reckon we can settle your mind on that score, ma'am,' Wes said turning his glance on Ben. 'Tag!'

A smile flickered across Ben's face.

'Been thinking the same myself.'

'Tag?' She brushed the tears from her eyes

and looked puzzled.

'Taggart J. Brodie,' Wes elaborated and Stumpy let out a whoop that had them all looking at the old-timer.

'Tag Brodie,' Stumpy said. 'You boys kin get Tag Brodie?' There was almost awe in his voice as he said the name.

'He owes us a favour or two,' Ben admitted.

'Then you ain't got no problem, Miss Angie,' Stumpy declared happily.

'I'd like a share in this joy, Wes,' Angie pointed out.

'Ol' Tag is the meanest, orneriest trail boss that ever rode the range. Him and his boys'd take a herd to hell and back if the notion took 'em and they'd face the devil himself if he stood in their way.'

'That's the pure truth,' Ben agreed.

'Well how do we get this wonder-man?' Angie asked.

'Ben and me, we'll take a ride into town after supper and see if we can't set it up,' Wes offered.

The day was a pink flush on the western horizon as the two rode into Freedom. Shadow and darkness was already beginning to merge into one, but light flared from windows on either side of the wide, dusty mainstreet forming a checkered pattern of light and shadow that the two rode through.

Elroy Gibbens at the telegraph office looked up as the door opened, disapproval on his thin, bony features. He was all set to close up for the night and pulled a fat-bodied watch from the pocket of his dark vest.

'Sorry, gents, we're closed. Come back in the morning,' he snapped in his reedy voice. Elroy was a man of habit and hated having his habits disturbed. Right now he should be heading towards the boarding-house where supper would be waiting.

Wes leaned on the counter smiling.

'Well that's just fine by us. You see I know how to use one of those things and what I have to send is private. How's about you attend your usual business and come back here in an hour or so?'

Elroy was scandalized at the very thought of what the stranger was saying. He recognized the two from the stories that had come out of Clancey's saloon.

'Can't rightly do that. This is government property and only to be used by a government appointed agent. I'll send your message, but it's gotta be quick.' He figured it would not be a smart thing to antagonize the two. Especially the big one whose head was almost lost in the shadows of the ceiling.

'Like I said,' Wes returned cordially. 'It's meant to be a surprise. I wouldn't want it let out accidental-like what's been sent.'

Elroy swallowed uneasily.

'This is govern...' He ended with a startled yelp that all but cleared up the touch of constipation that he had been suffering from of late as a big hand buried the point of a knife deep in the wooden counter-top before him. His eyes popped glassily as he looked up with white-faced terror into the unsmiling eyes of Ben Travis. The upward throw of the light from the lamp carved dark, merciless shadows into Ben's face.

'I hate make a nuisance of myself, friend,' Wes said. 'But it is kinda important and my pard's getting impatient.'

Elroy's prominent Adam's apple jigged in his throat and he nodded his head.

'Have it ... have it,' he squeaked. 'I get paid to send messages not to get killed.' Sweat shone on his face.

'That's real neighbourly of you.' Wes walked around the counter to a door at the rear. This opened into a tiny storeroom with a small, barred, single window set high in one wall and no other exits. 'Be obliged if'n you'd step this way, Mister...?'

'Gibbens, Elroy Gibbens,' Elroy stammered out.

'This way, Elroy. Soon as we've finished you can come out and lock up.'

Elroy nodded dumbly, jumped up and fled through the door.

Ben pulled his knife free from the counter.

'I hate scaring innocent folk like that,' he complained.

'All in a good cause, big fella,' Wes replied as he took up position before the sender and began tapping the key. Twenty minutes later he had an answer and smiled triumphantly at Ben.

'Tag and his boys'll be here in two days. Let's give ol' Elroy his freedom and we can be on our way.'

'Sounds good to me,' Ben replied.

Elroy breathed a sigh of relief as a few moments later Wes helped him on with his coat.

'I'd be obliged if this little bit o' business is kept between ourselves. Here's ten dollars to cover the use of your government property and ten dollars more for the inconvenience to your good self. I hope we understand each other or the big fella here might get a mite tetchy and you wouldn't like that.' He thrust the greenbacks into Elroy's hand.

'No, sir, no sir,' Elroy spluttered as he stared at the money in his hand. He had half expected to have his throat cut, not to be paid. 'I mean, yes ... sir no sir...' Elroy was getting confused and Wes clapped him on the back.

'I can see you understand,' he said. Minutes later Elroy extinguished the lamp and followed the two out into the night. They were standing either side of Elroy as the man turned from locking the door. He was pocketing the key when the bullet caught him high on the left and shattered his heart on its way through. He was dead before he hit the ground.

THREE

Joe Santos had seen the two ride into town. He had paused on the sidewalk across the street from Clancey's to light a cigarette. Delicious memories of the voluptuous Rose whose charms he had been sampling only moments before vanished. He stepped back into the shadows and watched as they passed by. He remained watching until he saw them rein in at the telegraph office and enter. Cigarette forgotten for the moment he had crossed the street and hurried into the saloon.

Billy Redland and Smiley were bellied up against one end of the long counter and Billy's scowl became a nasty grin as he listened to Joe.

'Then we'uns got the bastards,' Billy said in a low voice.

'Hey, the boss said to do nothing,' Smiley pointed out recognizing the grin as meaning trouble.

'No two-bit drifter's gonna make me eat dirt and get away with it. This is personal.' Billy flicked a quick look around. The saloon was noisy and busy, Clancey at the far end of the counter. He tossed back his drink. 'Finish up,' he ordered to Smiley. 'We got some business to attend to.'

The three slipped through a rear door and out into a side alley. Joe grabbed Billy's arm.

'What's going on, Billy? What you aiming to do?' he asked in alarm.

'Give them boys a surprise that'll put some work the undertaker's way,' Billy replied ominously.

'What if we're seen?' Smiley spoke up.

'It's dark ain't it?' Billy cried. 'We'll take 'em from the alley across the street from the telegraph office then hightail it back here. By the time folks realize what's happened we'll be sitting pretty. They're strangers. Ain't no one gonna worry too much.

C'mon, time's a-wasting.'

They were ready and waiting in the alley by the time Wes and Ben with Elroy emerged from the darkened office.

As the first bullet slammed the unfortunate Elroy back against the door he had just locked a whole fusillade of shots rang out. Wes and Ben dived in opposite directions as the window by the door shattered. The two horses whickered in alarm as the bullets buzzed around them.

Wes had drawn his Peacemaker as he hit the boards of the sidewalk and loosed off a couple of quick shots in the direction of the red muzzle flashes. Billy, seeing that the element of surprise was gone called out to the others.

'Let's get out of here.'

Joe and Smiley did not argue and together the three ran down the alley and vanished into the backlots behind the buildings. People had appeared in the street, faces pointing in the direction of the telegraph office. Wes heard booted feet running and hauled himself up, fragments of glass falling from his body.

'They're gone,' he called. Ben had heard their escape and was already crouched at the sprawled Elroy's side.

'He's dead,' he announced grimly as Sheriff Caulder lumbered up, a scattergun clasped in his hands, the butt jammed against his paunchy stomach.

'What the hell's going on here?' he demanded eyes drifting to the dead Elroy and back on to the two.

'Somebody tried to kill us, Sheriff and poor Elroy happened to be in the way. The dirty bushwhackers were in yonder alley. We heard them take off running,' Wes cried.

'Did you get a sight of them?' Caulder asked.

'If'n I had, Sheriff, they'd be dead by now,' Wes replied grimly.

'How many do you reckon?'

'Two, three maybe.' Wes looked across at Ben.

'Seems about right,' Ben agreed stonily.

'I'd appreciate you boys coming to my office to make a statement.'

'We'd be obliged to, Sheriff. Elroy was good enough to help us and we'd sure like to get the ones that did this,' Wes said.

Caulder barked out a few gruff orders and as the crowd dispersed, the excitement of the night over, two men moved forward to take the body away.

It was thirty minutes later that Caulder marched into the saloon with Wes and Ben in tow. He glanced around with fierce, dark eyes from beneath grey, tangled eyebrows. Pushing into his fifties, Caulder was still a force to be reckoned with. His glance settled on Billy Redland and his two cronies seated at a table by the side wall. He headed towards them an expectant silence settling through the saloon.

'Been a shooting in town. Man's dead,' Caulder barked out as he faced Billy across the table.

'What's that got to do with us, Sheriff?' Billy asked.

'Let me see your guns,' Caulder ordered bringing the short barrelled scattergun up. By now Wes and Ben had arranged themselves either side of the table. Billy eyed them.

'New deputies, Sheriff?'

'The guns. All of you,' Caulder thundered.

Billy grinned and drew his weapon.

'Ain't no need for that, Sheriff.'

'On the table.'

Still grinning Billy laid his gun down and the others followed suit. Caulder examined each one.

'They've been fired recently.'

'That's the pure truth, Sheriff,' Billy agreed easily. 'Boys and I took a few shots at a jack-rabbit on the way into town. The darn critter got away. It sure did move.' He chuckled at the memory.

Both Wes and Ben saw the look of relief that chased the anxiety from Smiley and Joe's eyes.

'That's right, Sheriff,' Joe backed up.

'Some law agin it, Sheriff?' Billy asked

innocently. 'Has the critter come in and made a complaint?' He laughed at his joke and the other two joined in.

'Have you been here all the evening?' Caulder asked.

'Drinking Clancey's watered-down whiskey,' Billy vouched.

Caulder glared at them.

'Clancey, get over here,' he roared, not taking his eyes from the smiling Billy. 'Have these boys been here all the evening?'

'Far as I know, Sheriff. Hell it's busy in here. I don't see who comes and goes.' Clancey arrived, his big face decorated with bushy side whiskers. 'Anyone can leave and come back and I wouldn't know. Is that all, Sheriff?'

Caulder nodded and Clancey moved away.

'We did pop out back for a leak, Sheriff,' Billy said.

'All together I suppose?'

'Hell, it's dark out there, Sheriff. Ain't no telling who might be lurking.' The grin fell from Billy's face. 'You accusing us of something, Sheriff? If so best you come out and say it.'

'Just pursuing an enquiry.'

'So we're not accused of anything?' Billy persisted.

'Not at the moment,' Caulder agreed heavily and Billy threw a sly, triumphant glance at the two. 'But I'll be keeping an eye on you three.'

'Makes me feel plumb safe, Sheriff, knowing you'll be watching over me and the boys so we'uns come to no harm,' Billy smirked.

'Don't get smart with me, Redland,' Caulder snarled. He looked at Wes. 'If'n you remember anything be sure and let me know.' With that Caulder turned and stomped away, vanishing through the batwings into the night. His departure heralded the return of the saloon to normal as the piano struck a chord.

Wes glared down at Billy.

'There ain't no doubt in my mind that you

killed Elroy trying to get Ben and me.' He spoke softly, but each man heard the words crystal clear. 'You boys walk real soft from now on because I'll be looking out for you.'

'Make that we,' Ben added, stony-eyed.

It was two days later. Angela was tending the vegetable patch in a wild area out back of the house when Willy loped up.

'Riders coming, Miss Angie. Twenty, thirty maybe. Real mean looking bodies,' he yelled.

She felt a chill spread through her. Wes and Ben had gone out to the north range while Stumpy had taken the wagon into town.

'Clayburn's men?'

'Ain't regular Circle C riders, ma'am.' Willy looked scared. She drew a deep breath and tossed the hoe aside grabbing up a Winchester resting against a tree stump before heading towards the front gate.

It had been quiet, too quiet for too long. Since the night that Wes and Ben had been attacked in town and Elroy Gibbens killed, an uneasy calm had settled over the land. It had felt to her like the itchy calm before the storm. Now the storm had broken. She heard the thunder of hooves as she approached the gate and saw a ragged line of men sweeping down the southern slope towards them. Willy had diverted to the bunkhouse only to reappear seconds later clutching Stumpy's shotgun. He limped to Angela's side and stood tight-lipped and ready.

An icy wash of dread flowed over Angela's body and tingled on her flesh as the line of riders reined to a halt. The animals they rode tossed their heads and snorted and seemed to have the same evil sparkle that their owners had. Clad in drab, sombre garb, hard eyes stared from weathered, stubble-ringed faces. Hostile, merciless faces. Her mouth grew dry as a rider on a blood bay kneed his mount forward. He looked as old as time. Flesh dry and leathery and carved with deep lines. From dark, bony sockets fringed with tangled grey, dark eyes stared broodingly out. A downward curving, grey moustache curled from his upper lip and joined the stubble of his chin.

'Who are you? What do you want?' she called nervously.

'You aiming to use that, girl?' The voice was gravel thick.

Angela licked her lips.

'If I have to,' Angela said tautly and levered a shell into the breech, raising the rifle to cover the man.

A smile flickered for an instant on the carved features. The man showed no fear as he regarded her coolly.

'Ain't a friendly way to greet a body, girl,' he observed.

'Depends just how friendly you are,' she countered. 'Now state your business or ride on.'

Her finger tightened on the trigger.

'You can put up the gun, ma'am.'

Angela almost fainted with relief at the sound of Wes's voice. She turned her head to see both him and Ben riding between the men and the fence. The grizzled-faced man eyed the approaching two with no apparent change of expression until at the last moment his face split in a grin.

'Howdy, boys,' he greeted. His eyes slid to Angela. 'Feisty little piece ain't she?'

Wes and Ben grinned at the words and her face flamed.

'What's going on, here?'

'Miss Angie, meet Taggart J. Brodie.'

Her face flushed a deeper red.

'I'm sorry, Mr Brodie. Willy get the gate open.'

'The name's Tag, girl. My pa was Mr Brodie.' Tag slid from his horse. The rest of his crew had broken their line formation and were coming forward to greet Wes and Ben like long-lost brothers. Wes slid from his horse and walked through the gate with Tag. The man was a head shorter than Wes, but there was nothing small about the way he carried himself. Self-assurance exuded from every pore.

'Seems you mentioned trouble in your

message?' Tag directed at Wes.

'Just a kindly neighbour who doesn't want to see Miss Angie's cows get to market.'

Tag eyed Angela. 'Well you got no problems on that score now, girl. Ain't worked for no woman afore,' he remarked.

'Now don't go telling her ranching's a man's work or she's just as likely to up and run you off the range,' Wes said with a gleam in his eyes.

'I can appreciate that,' Tag agreed.

'Thank you for coming, Tag.' She steered away from the male/female battle, still blushing. To cover her confusion she eyed the bunkhouse. 'I don't know how we're gonna put all your men up. The bunkhouse is only fit one end...'

'Pay no mind, girl. I'll allow that Wes here has found us a choice campsite.'

'North range. Ben and I checked it out this morning. Good place to gather the cows too. They's a mite spread about at the moment.'

'Seen 'em. Three, four days to get 'em

rounded up and by that time Shorty should be here with the chuck-wagon and we can be on our way.'

Tag Brodie's arrival had not gone unnoticed. A rider sped away to the west hidden by low hills. Hoyt Green had spent a while drifting about the west until joining up with the Circle C. He was a top hand when it came to cows and this he had learned riding with Tag Brodie. He galloped into the yard and leapt from the still-moving horse.

Milt Clayburn was walking a white stallion in a small corral and being watched by Billy Redland, Smiley and Joe when Hoyt arrived in rapid fashion. Clayburn jerked his head around.

'Trouble, boss. The Parsons girl's got herself a crew to round-up her cows.'

A look of annoyance crossed Clayburn's face. It might be the influence of the two new hands. So far he had done nothing about them, still waiting a reply from McCloud in Laramie, but the situation now required something be done and done quick.

He dropped the tether and lithely climbed the rail, gesturing to a stable-hand to take over.

'Then something must be done to discourage these men.'

'Not these ones, boss.' Hoyt shook his head. 'It's Tag Brodie.' Even the smile on Billy's face faltered.

'You sure?' Billy demanded.

'Rode with him for two years. I'm sure,' Hoyt replied.

Milt looked thoughtful. He too had heard of Tag Brodie. The man's reputation was legend and the men that rode with him were hard and ruthless.

'You've lost this round, boss,' Billy commented and Clayburn's face hardened.

'Maybe not,' he said thoughtfully, then, 'Get into town. Find out what that fool McCloud is doing. Get me a reply about those two and quick.'

'Sure, boss.' His abortive murder attempt on the two that had resulted in the death of the telegraph man, Billy had kept to himself. Clayburn didn't appreciate initiative that failed.

Clayburn watched the three depart and turned his mind to the immediate problem. The answer when it came to him was so simple he wondered why he had not thought of it before. He chuckled to himself. Let the girl think she had the upper hand for a few days. Let this Brodie do all the hard work, then drop his surprise.

In the dawn light of a day a week later Angela stood at the gate with the rest of the Boxed P crew, including Martha, to watch the herd depart.

In that week, Tag Brodie and his crew of drovers had worked wonders. The herd had been rounded up, unmarked animals branded. The chuck-wagon and remuda had arrived. Wes and Ben had joined in the round-up, working like demons in a whirlwind of activity that made Angela almost forget about the Circle C. Almost, that was, until Clayburn and Sheriff Caulder with an unhappy-looking Jethro Potts, the manager of Freedom's only bank, rode out of the dawn mist. Angela was so excited, her eyes were on the bellowing herd, that she did not see the visitors until the last moment.

'Sheriff, Mr Potts.' There was surprise in her voice at seeing the podgy bank manager. Clayburn she ignored though she could not ignore the smirk on the man's face. Alarm bells began to ring in her head. Wes and Ben edged closer to Angela in an unconscious, protective move.

'Ma'am,' Caulder greeted heavily as though being here was weighing down hard on him.

'What can I do for you?' Angela asked nervously.

'Potts,' Caulder growled.

Potts licked his lips.

'I'm s ... sorry, Miss Parsons, but ... but...'

'What this bumbling fool is trying to say,' Clayburn intervened, kneeing his mount forward, 'is that I have taken up the option on your grandfather's loan. You are now payable to me and I'm calling in your marker.' Clayburn's smirk grew. 'You owe me five thousand dollars, Miss Parsons. Now I'm a reasonable man. You have until noon today to come up with the money or I take possession of the Boxed P and it's all legal.'

FOUR

Angela, dumbfounded at the news, felt a numb helplessness wash over her. All the hard work and effort

'You can't do that,' she protested weakly.

'Show her the documents, Potts,' Clayburn instructed through a gloating smile. She ignored the proffered documents.

'I'll have the money as soon as the herd is sold.'

'My herd you mean.' Clayburn was enoying himself. 'If you can't come up with the money the herd's mine too along with everything else. Sheriff, as the law hereabouts it's up to you to make sure this herd stays where it's at.'

'Sheriff?' Angela pleaded.

'I don't need you to tell me my job, Clayburn,' Caulder said roughly to the man then looked down at Angela. 'Sorry, ma'am. I gotta go along with what Clayburn says. He has legal and binding documents. I'm sorry.' It was plain he did not like what he was being forced to do.

'Five thousand dollars, in cash, at the bank by noon,' Clayburn said.

'Cash!' Angela felt her world collapsing about her.

'You should have sold out when you had the chance. Now I get the Boxed P real cheap. Ranching's a man's world, Miss Parsons and you've learnt it the hard way.'

Angela stumbled away and clutched at the gate upright, hot tears blurring her vision. Tag Brodie rode alongside Clayburn, his face hard. During the week Angela had made quite a hit with Tag and his crew. Helping or trying to help, but always game to go on if she failed. To see her now being treated in this way was like a red rag to a bull to Tag and his crew. There was more than one calloused hand resting itchily on a gun butt.

'I don't like you, mister and when Tag Brodie gets a dislike for a person that said person had better mind his manners and stay outta my way.'

'You don't frighten me, Brodie. You heard him, Sheriff, he threatened me.'

Tag threw a look at Caulder.

'Howdy, Jeb.'

'Tag,' Caulder responded.

'You know each other? How nice,' Clayburn said. 'It still doesn't alter the fact that I was threatened by this man.'

'I didn't hear no threat. Just a man speaking his mind,' Caulder replied mildly.

'How come you're siding with this slick-tongued, toad, Jeb?' Tag asked.

'Sometimes you have to do things the law says is right even if they stink,' Caulder replied.

'Very good, Sheriff,' Clayburn applauded darkly. 'Just you make sure the herd stays put or I'll throw in a charge of cattle-rustling against Brodie here.'

Tag's face turned purple and Wes thought

it was time to step in and cool the situation.

'You've said your piece, Clayburn. Now get the hell out of here while you can or you may not live long enough to collect your blood money.'

'I'll see you in the bank at noon, Miss Parsons. You'll need to be signing a few papers that Potts here will have ready and waiting for you. Come on, Potts, there's work to be done. Remember, Sheriff, I'm holding you responsible for the herd.' With that Clayburn wheeled his horse and urged it forward. Potts followed, relieved to be on his way. Angela turned away, eyes brimming and almost ran back towards the house bathed in the light of the rising sun. Tag's face was bleak as he eyed Caulder.

'I jus' hope you can sleep well at nights, Jeb,' he said caustically. 'That little girl busted her butt helping me and the boys. She deserves better'n the mean, low-down trick Clayburn pulled.'

'I don't like it any more than you, but I stick by the law and Clayburn's got it on his side for the moment. Don't move the herd, Tag.' Caulder turned his horse and cantered away. Tag watched him go, anger burning in his hard, dark eyes and slapped one hand into the other.

'What'll we do about this, Wes?' He turned to the younger man helplessly.

'Don't be too hard on the sheriff, Tag. I get the feeling he's good people. He don't like what Clayburn's doing any more than we do.'

Tag grinned sourly.

'Hell, I know that. Jeb Caulder and I grew up together in Cheyenne. I ain't holding nothin' agin him. It's that Clayburn fella, he needs a good stomping.'

Pete Cable, Tag's ramrod came forward.

'How's about we take the boys and teach that fella some manners, Tag?' His suggestion brought growls of approval from other members of the crew who had witnessed the scene, but Wes raised a staying hand.

'Hold on that, Pete. I'll allow it sounds a good idea, but it's not the way this time.

Rest easy until noon, Tag. We'll play this Clayburn's way. Maybe we can surprise that hombre some.'

Ben had followed Angela and found her out on the back porch of the house staring red-eyed at the mountains. She used a hand to wipe the tears from her face and forced a rueful smile.

'Guess this isn't the way ranchers carry on,' she said.

'I've seen growed men cry afore,' Ben said softly. 'Ranching men too.'

'I tried so hard, Ben, and nearly made it.' She gave a wry, drawn smile. 'I guess that in the end I took on more than I could handle.'

'You had no idea Clayburn would pull a low trick like that.'

'I should have figured it out. Now I've lost everything.'

'You ain't lost yet, ma'am,' Ben pointed out quietly. 'Not until noon.'

She looked up into the big man's calm face. The determination showed therein had a steadying effect on her.

'Still the optimist, eh, Ben?'

'All I know is that you shouldn't give up.'

Angela could get little comfort from those words as noon approached and she entered the bank with Wes and Ben. Billy Redland along with his two shadows were lounging about outside the bank when they arrived and Billy's face split in a wide grin.

'Reckon me and the boys'll sleep real easy up at the Boxed P tonight,' he gloated and seconds later lay full stretch on the sidewalk wondering where the mule that had kicked him came from. Through blurred vision all he could see was the form of Ben Travis looming over him.

Wes looked at Ben.

'Now was that a nice thing to do to poor Billy?' he chided mockingly.

'Yep,' Ben replied.

Milt Clayburn with Sheriff Caulder were waiting when the three entered.

'I like punctuality,' Clayburn said, glancing at the big clock on the side wall. 'A few minutes early too. I take it you have the money?'

'You know damn well I haven't,' Angela grated and Clayburn pursed his lips in exaggerated shock.

'My, my, such language,' he remarked, smiling all the more. Angela thought that if he smiled any wider he'd swallow his head. 'Potts bring the deeds over and we'll get this concluded. You realize I shall want you off of the Boxed P by sunset or I'll have the sheriff arrest you for trespass.' The remark brought a murderous glare from the silent Caulder.

'I wouldn't be too sure of that, Clayburn,' Wes drawled and became the centre of attention.

Clayburn lost his smile to a frown.

'What are you playing at, Hardiman?' He stared at the younger man through narrowed eyes. There was an inner laughter about him that instantly worried Clayburn.

'Noon you said,' Wes would not be hurried. 'And there's still a minute to go.'

'I don't know what you're up to, Hardiman, but the sheriff's here,' Clayburn pointed out.

'Wouldn't have it any other way,' Wes replied and his eyes flickered to the clock again. 'Thirty seconds to noon, Clayburn.' He had entered the bank with a saddle-bag over his shoulder. Removing it he opened one compartment and up-ended it on the counter. A wad of hundred-dollar bills thudded on to the wooden surface, raising dust motes to float lazily in a shaft of sunlight. 'Five thousand dollars in cash and it's still not noon.' There were still some fifteen seconds to go on the bank clock.

'Well I'll be...' Jeb Caulder breathed and for the first time that day a smile spread across his face.

At the Boxed P Tag Brodie eyed his watch and as the second hand slid across the twelve, half raised himself from the saddle and hollered,

'Move 'em out!'

At the bank Ben eyed the clock.

'Tag's on his way with your herd, ma'am,' he said to a stunned, speechless Angela.

'Sheriff,' Wes spoke up with a grin, 'I'd like

you to witness that Clayburn here signs the marker over to Miss Angie. Gotta keep it legal-like.'

'Be a pure pleasure,' Caulder agreed. 'Knowing as how Mr Clayburn is so hot on seeing that the law is carried out.'

'Where did you get that money?' Clayburn gripped the edge of the counter, his voice a dry, hoarse, rasp in the warm, still air of the bank.

'I'm a careful saver.'

'Thrifty as a squirrel,' Ben agreed. He took hold of Clayburn's coat front as he spoke and hauled him along the counter. 'I'd be obliged if you'd sign the marker as being paid in full, Mr Clayburn and then we can all get about our business.'

Outside the bank a few minutes later Caulder was still chuckling to himself.

'I gotta hand it to you, boys. You are full of surprises. But if I was you I'd watch my back from now on. Clayburn don't make a good enemy.'

'Neither do we, Sheriff,' Wes replied. 'And

reckon you should take your own advice.'

Since the five thousand dollars had dropped on to the counter in the bank, Angela had been reduced to a dumb spectator. One minute her world had been in ruins, the next, miraculously, it had been rebuilt.

'I don't know what to say.' She spoke for the first time as Caulder stomped back to his office. There was no sign of Milt Clayburn or his men.

'No need to say anything, Miss Angie,' Wes replied, grinning. 'I kinda enjoyed it.'

'That was some play, little fella,' Ben cracked. 'Counting the seconds like that.'

'Figured Clayburn had had his fun, so it was our turn.'

'I'll pay you back as soon as the herd's sold,' Angela said quickly, eyes shining.

'Whenever,' Wes replied expansively.

She looked at them both with fondness. She had never met anyone like these two before. They treated her as an equal and never talked down to her because she was a woman in a man's world. On impulse she swung on each man in turn and gave them a kiss on the cheek.

'You could have told me what you were planning.'

'If'n I had you'd have gone into yonder bank with a smile a mile wide and Clayburn would have known something was up. Sorry, ma'am,' Wes said and Angela laughed.

'It was worth it.' She climbed up on to the wagon seat and the two men settled either side of her, Ben taking up the reins and minutes later they were rolling out of town.

'How'd you reckon Tag got on taking the north-west trail?' Ben suddenly called across to Wes.

'North-west?' Angela was quick to take up his words. 'That leads to the Circle C.' She looked puzzled.

'Just a gesture to Elroy's memory,' Wes said. 'Sure hope nothing gets in the way.'

The Circle C ranch house was a showpiece of southern-style elegance in the wild,

Wyoming prairie. Built along the lines of a cotton baron's mansion, a three-tier structure of white and black ringed with triple verandas, high-peaked roofs with low, square turrets at each corner and tall windows. It rose from a bed of ornate gardens and soft, green lawns to ooze wealth and splendour like a jewel on a multi-hued, velvet cushion. Just now the cushion looked a mite tatty.

Fifteen hundred head of cattle on the prod are no respectors of the finer things of life. The ornate gardens and lawns lay in churned up ruins and once white fences had been reduced to matchwood. A herd of Clayburn's prize horses had been scattered and eight of his men nursed an assortment of injuries gathered when they tried to stop the herd.

Milt Clayburn listened in wordless rage as one of the luckless hands told of the Boxed P herd being driven across the land. After being out-manoeuvred at the bank, the devastation that greeted his eyes did little to improve his disposition.

'But we done caught one of them Boxed P hands skulking on the ridge when the herd had gone through,' the man ended. 'Hog-tied him in the barn.'

Milt Clayburn's eyes gleamed.

'Bring him here.'

A few minutes later the slight form of Willy stood shaking before Milt Clayburn.

'The gimpy kid from the livery,' Billy spat. 'What were you doing on Mr Clayburn's property, kid?'

'J ... just w ... watching. I didn't do nothing.' Willy was terrified. When Tag had moved the herd out he had followed at a distance, pretending to be part of the drive, pretending to be a drover. He had paused on the low ridge and watched dumbfounded as the herd tore through the Circle C spread. He didn't understand why Tag had brought the herd this way; he figured he must have made a mistake, but even so he got a savage satisfaction seeing the destruction. Milt Clayburn had made Miss Angie cry and for that he hated him. It was while he was on the ridge that two of Clayburn's riders found him and took him back to the ranch.

'Just watching were you?' Clayburn hissed through clenched teeth as the anger within him rose and centred on the unfortunate youth. He lashed out with the back of an open hand, with a blow that sent Willy sprawling in the churned-up earth, blood erupting from a split lip.

'Want we should maybe stomp the boy a little?' Billy offered, leering down at the near-to-tears youngster.

'What he needs to do is take a real close look,' Clayburn said softly. 'Get a rope, Billy.' He smiled nastily at Willy.

'What you gonna do?' Willy asked fearfully, scrambling into a sitting position as Smiley and Joe moved in to flank him. 'Please, Mr Clayburn, don't hurt me.'

'It's too late for that, boy,' Clayburn breathed. 'I'm hurting real bad at what those Boxed P cattle did to my home.'

Billy arrived with the rope and one end was fastened about Willy's ankles. The other end Clayburn wrapped a few turns about the silver saddlehorn of his horse's saddle as he climbed up.

'Please, Mr Clayburn,' Willy cried out.

'Take a look, boy, a real, good look. If'n the Boxed P want trouble then they've got it and you can deliver the message.' Clayburn dug his heels hard into the horse's flanks and set the beast galloping back and forth over the torn up ground, dragging the unfortunate Willy behind.

FIVE

While Clayburn dragged the screaming youngster behind his horse, Angela had Ben stop the wagon on the rise overlooking the valley. She had been thoughtfully silent as the journey progressed and both men could guess what was running though her mind.

'You're not ordinary cowboys are you?' she said after a moment's silence. 'I mean ordinary cowboys don't ride about with five thousand dollars looking for work.' She stared ahead at the distant mountains as she spoke.

Wes threw Ben a look behind Angela's head, a half smile on his face.

'Guess we do owe you an explanation seeing as how the business at the bank kinda forced our hand, but you might not like it.'

She turned and fixed him with her green eyes.

'Try me,' she offered.

'Might be an idea to stretch our legs,' Wes suggested. 'It could take a while.'

'Well?' she prompted a few minutes later seated on a grassy knoll. Wes stood before her while Ben lounged against the wagon chewing on a grass stem.

''Bout a year ago a shipment of gold *en route* to the rail-head at Casper, vanished. It came from the proceeds of a dozen mining camps in the mountains where it had been shipped to a central point, smelted into bars and packed into crates ready for the wagon trip to Casper.'

'How much was it worth?' she asked.

'Million dollars give or take,' Ben answered casually and her eyes widened.

'That's a lot of temptation to put in a single wagon,' she said.

'That's how it turned out,' Wes agreed. 'Escorted by a cavalry unit under the leadership of a Major Phillips, the whole kit and caboodle vanished after leaving Freedom, and whole means whole. The escort, the horses they rode, the wagon, everything. It was as though it had never existed. Teams of men scoured this area for six months before we came on the scene. Ben and I work for the government and until this business is sorted, the Treasury Department.' Wes broke off to let her absorb the startling information.

'And you still think it can be found after all this time?'

'I'm betting on it, ma'am. You see there have been no big gold deposits registered since the robbery, which means that it's being held somewhere. A mighty patient man planned this robbery and he's willing to wait a year or two, maybe more afore he starts getting rid of it.'

'He's also a mightly clever hombre,' Ben joined in. 'The bars of gold had a special stamp mark. One bar turned up in El Paso eight months ago and another in Ruidosa on the Mex border six months back. Figure he's trying to give the impression the gold's been spread around.'

'How do you know it hasn't?' Angela asked.

'Because it's here, ma'am,' Wes took over.

'Here?' Angela threw both men astonished stares.

'More to the point, hidden somewhere on Boxed P land.'

'I don't understand,' she said coming to her feet. 'How can it be here?' Her gaze flicked from man to man. Wes smiled at her alarm and confusion, took her arms and gently forced her to sit again.

'Sit down, ma'am and I'll try and explain,' he placated. 'The odd bar of gold that was found dragged Ben and I on several wild goose chases and then we got to thinking, why had Major Phillips ordered the wagon to leave Freedom in the middle of the night? You might argue that travelling at night was safer. Less likely to be seen. You might argue that the major had another reason, a crooked reason, so we followed that line of thought and did some digging into the major's background.'

'Seems he was a man with a powerful dislike of the army life of late with young officers coming up through the ranks and passing him in the promotion stakes,' Ben took up the story. 'He also had a liking for women, gambling and whiskey. Three powerful ways to part a man from his money and get his mind to wondering how he can get more – money that is – easier than working for it. Found out that once a month he took a trip to Laramie to play in a card game. A high stakes card game. Two other regulars of the card game turned out to be Milt Clayburn and your grandfather, Frank Parsons.'

'Now we had a convenient tie-in,' Wes continued. 'Frank, Clayburn, the major and the gold disappearing between Freedom and Casper. Sometimes two and two don't make four, but this time we reckon it does. The major was in to Clayburn for a sizeable amount. The gold shipment was a way out for him to repay his debts and have plenty left for a happy old age. It didn't matter that nine men had to die in the process and if you include the major himself, ten, but then the major never included himself.'

'How do you know he's dead?' Angela asked.

'It might have been the major's idea at the beginning, but Clayburn and your grandfather refined it. They were prepared to wait for a couple of years. The major was a 'now' person. He would've wanted his cut straight away and that spelt danger to the others. I don't know how many were involved in the ambush and subsequent disappearance, but we reckon it was more than your grandfather and Clayburn. Whoever it was could afford to wait. Phillips was the only weak link and they had to dispose of him.'

'But it's still all hearsay and supposition,' Angela objected. 'It doesn't prove that the gold is here or ever was here.'

'True, ma'am,' Ben said. 'That was until Clayburn started his campaign to get his hands on the Boxed P. It was then it all came together. Frank Parsons and Clayburn were friends and partners in the robbery. They shared the responsibilities. One hid the gold, the other got rid of the wagon, horses and bodies. We figure the gold was stashed on the Boxed P and it's at this point that things get a mite hazy. Clayburn had the chance to move the gold before you arrived and he didn't. After you arrived, he couldn't.'

Angela shook her head.

'I don't understand.'

'Neither do we, ma'am,' Wes continued, vexed. 'There was a month between Frank dying and you turning up, we checked that. Plenty of time to move the gold to a new location. Instead he waits for you to arrive and stirs up trouble that's bound to get him noticed.' He shook his head. 'Don't make sense.'

'Maybe you're making something out of nothing,' she suggested. 'Could be he's just after the land and he and grandfather had no part in the robbery?'

'It's a possibility,' Wes conceded. 'And

that's why we signed up with you. Figured to do a little looking to make sure, but then Clayburn's play with the bank marker kinda forced us into the open.'

'You realize that Clayburn will be wondering how you came up with the money?' she pointed out.

'It had crossed our mind,' Ben said. 'Might be better for you if you spent a few days in town. Things might get a tad lively around here.'

'Not on your life,' she said stoutly, coming to her feet. 'It's my ranch now and I'll fight for it.' She glared from one to the other, daring them to disagree. Wes smiled across at Ben.

'Proddy as a mossy-horn,' he muttered, then louder, 'Can't throw you off, ma'am, but we'd be obliged you kept who we are and why we're here to yourself. Word gets out that there's gold buried on your land and you won't see the grass for gold hunters. That means Martha, Stumpy and Willy.'

'They won't hear it from me,' she promised. 'Well, let's get to the ranch. I can't wait to tell the others the good news.'

Willy's non-appearance was pushed to the background by the news Angela had to tell, then Stumpy had to relay how Tag got the herd underway. Wes and Ben, preoccupied with pondering the whereabouts of the missing gold, gave Willy little thought until much later when Stumpy brought up the subject.

'You boys seen the kid about?' he voiced as he came upon the two in the barn by the corral.

'Thought he was with you,' Ben said.

'Ain't see'd 'im all the afternoon,' Stumpy said worriedly. He had taken the youngster under his wing. The boy was a good listener and seemed to appreciate Stumpy's wealth of tall stories.

'Thought he was tending the horses in the north pasture, but he ain't there; and another thing, his horse is gone.'

The men exchanged glances. Outside the late afternoon shadows were lengthening towards evening.

'Maybe he rode a-ways with Tag?' Ben suggested. 'He was mighty taken with Tag and his boys. Reckon I'll saddle up and take a ride.'

'We'll both go,' Wes said. 'Stumpy tell Miss Angie what we're doing.'

Blood ran down the horse's flanks, staining its tan coat, but it came not from the beast itself, but the rider sprawled forward on its neck.

Barely conscious, Willy managed to retain a double-handed grip on the bloodstained mane and hold on. The clothes about the youngster's body had been reduced to bloody tatters and dirt and blood mingled on the exposed, shredded flesh. Blood dribbled from his lips while pain screwed his lacerated face into a mask of agony. Every step the horse took jolted though his battered, mutilated body. Clayburn had dragged him back and forth across the churned-up ground until finally he, Willy, had passed out. When he had come to Billy Redland and his men were manhandling him on to his horse. He could remember their laughter as they slapped the horse's rump and sent it cantering away.

His vision was a green/blue blur that would not clear. He hoped the horse knew where it was going, for he didn't. He just clung and prayed. He knew that both legs were broken and the way his chest hurt he was busted some inside. Tears filled his eyes. He did not want to die!

Willy must have lost consciousness. The next thing he remembered was falling. He hit the ground in an explosion of pain and lay there for a moment on his back, unable to move as pain gripped and held him. When finally it had settled enough he managed to roll on to his front. He attempted to drag himself forward. The effort was too much. A bubbling cry of pain fell from his lips and he slid into darkness.

Wes and Ben found the bloody, huddled form thirty minutes later. They had come across the horse first with its ominously stained coat, the animal leisurely chewing grass. Willy lay in a dip a hundred yards away.

Ben's face was grim as he gently turned the boy over and Wes fetched a blanket to cover him.

'What happened, kid?' Ben asked gently as Willy's pain-glazed eyes flickered open.

'I didn't do nothin', Ben. I was just looking. I seen the herd plough straight across the grounds of Mr Clayburn's ranch...'

'We know, Willy,' Wes interrupted, hunkering down on the boy's other side. 'Did they see you looking?'

'Mr Clayburn got real mad.' The blood ran bright from the boy's lips and his flesh had taken on a waxy hue. 'He roped me behind his horse and dragged me over the ground.' Willy's face creased in pain and he began to cough. Ben eased him into a sitting position and glanced across at Wes, face hard. 'Then they put me on mah horse. Is it getting cold, Ben? I feel cold.'

'Night's coming on, boy. Get's cooler at night,' Ben replied.

Willy forced a smile.

'I can see that. It's getting real dark,' Willy agreed. 'Tag said the next time he's through here, he'd look to be taking me on as cook's louse, if'n I'd a mind too. I figure I'd like that.'

'Sure, Willy. Sounds good,' Ben agreed. 'Ol Tag could do with a boy like you, sure enough.'

'So cold,' Willy mumbled and it was as though a light in his eyes had been turned out. The eyes looked through and beyond Ben then Willy's head lolled to one side and his harsh, gurgling breathing stopped.

Ben laid the boy down and rose to his feet. Gone was the friendly, smiling face. Now the features were set hard and mean and Wes knew that all hell was about to break loose.

About the same time that Wes and Ben set out to look for Willy, a rider arrived at Milt Clayburn's Circle C. He handed Clayburn an envelope and after eyeing the torn up frontage of the ranch, he sped back to town, full of that news. The rider, Rance Bolten, did not work for Clayburn. He had been called upon to take a message that had come into the telegraph office from Laramie.

Milt Clayburn stood at the elegant french doors as the room behind him filled with darkness and read the message again.

THE TWO MEN IN QUESTION ARE GOVERNMENT AGENTS ran the message. It was signed, *McCLOUD*.

Clayburn screwed up the message and turned to his desk. Here, after lighting the oil lamp and a cigar, he bellowed for Billy Redland. He cursed Frank Parsons for dying in the first place and causing him this problem. The answer to the problem was simple enough. He would let the two agents find the gold for him and he knew just how to call the play.

'You want me, boss?' Billy entered the room.

'Send word to the Bodine brothers. I have

a job for them that pays a thousand dollars each for a night's work.' A smile played on Clayburn's face. 'Tell them they'll be having a woman for company.'

Billy looked blank for a moment then realization flooded in.

'The Parsons woman?' he said aghast.

'She won't be so high and mighty after a visit with them boys,' Clayburn chuckled and Billy felt a coldness wash over him.

'But the Bodines...?' Billy felt a shudder pass through him.

SIX

The setting sun painted the mountains red and black and threw long shadows from the trees as the two returned to the Boxed P with Willy draped over the saddle of his horse. Neither had said much on the return journey, but both were aware that Clayburn had upped the stakes and the game was going to get a mite hot from now on.

After laying Willy to rest in the big barn it was a morose group that gathered in the house for the meal that Martha had prepared, but appetites were low and food was only picked at.

'Clayburn can't be allowed to get away with murder,' Angela said hotly as later they gathered, just the three of them, in the parlour. They could hear Martha working in the kitchen. Stumpy had taken himself off to the bunkhouse. He and the kid had developed a bond and the boy's death had hit him hard. 'The sheriff...'

'Will not be able to do anything,' Wes cut in from where he stood at the end of a big, stone hearth. Over the hearth the wall was decorated with an Indian bow, a quiver of arrows and a tomahawk. 'Clayburn will be able to produce a dozen witnesses to say that he did not touch the boy and the only witness we have is dead.'

'So what do we do?'

'Don't worry, ma'am, Clayburn won't be getting away with anything,' Ben called icily from the depths of a big armchair. 'At the moment he's playing the cards. We'll just bide our time and wait for his next move.'

Milt Clayburn's next move came the following night. The day had been a sombre one. Wes had ridden with Angela into Freedom to inform Sheriff Caulder of Willy's death. His words echoed Ben's of the night before – without witnesses there was nothing he could do. So, after registering Willy's death, they returned to the ranch and in a stand of cottonwood on the north pasture, they buried Willy. It was here he had spent many happy evenings with Tag and his boys and Angela did not want him buried and forgotten in the town cemetery.

Later and until evening began to creep across the land, Wes and Ben spent their time roaming the outbuildings and the wooded area on the other side of the creek, looking and searching for a sign to show where the gold might be hidden. As they gathered for supper they knew that the hunt for the gold was not going to be an easy one. Frank Parsons had done his task well, maybe too well. Much later the three gathered in the comfortable parlour to drink coffee and discuss the possible whereabouts of the gold. There had been no mention or hint of reprisals against the Circle C. After the initial shock of Willy's barbaric death, they had let their rage simmer, especially Ben. They all knew that if they had ridden, guns blazing, on to Circle C property, Clayburn would have the law on his side with enough home-grown witnesses for them to all end up in the local jail. Revenge was not forgotten, merely put on hold.

The conversation had lagged as what seemed all possible places had been discussed and discarded.

'Can you smell smoke?' Angela asked suddenly, nose wrinkling.

Her question was answered by an agitated Martha bursting into the room.

'Miss Angie. The bunkhouse's on fire!'

Ben and Wes came to their feet, nerves taut, expecting something but not knowing what.

'Stumpy!' they said in unison.

Stumpy jerked from his whiskey-induced sleep and sat up on his bunk, tears running from smoke-stinging eyes. His action sent an empty bottle tumbling to the floor. For a second night he had taken a drink to Willy's memory and his head spun. The far end of the bunkhouse was on fire and black smoke funneling along the rafters reached out and wrapped him in a hazy, choking cocoon. Coughing and gagging, clad only in grubby long-johns, he tumbled from the bunk, intending to make for the door. He reached a centrally placed trestle table before a combination of heat, smoke and whiskey sent him to his knees. He managed to grab hold of the table and cling on as his head reeled and the room distorted and rocked sickeningly about him.

The orange and yellow flames licked the wooden walls, roaring and crackling, boards cracking explosively. With a supreme effort he hauled himself to his feet and staggered to the door only to find that it would not budge. He tugged frenziedly at the handle as claws of smoke reached with sharp, choking fingers deep into his lungs.

He beat at the door in helpless frustration as the heat from the flames singed the fabric of his long-johns and blistered his skin beneath. Aware now that his life expectancy could be measured in minutes Stumpy lurched away from the door towards a window, but in doing so he tangled with a chair and fell. His head hit the edge of the table and he slammed to the floor and lay still.

With the flames staining the Wyoming darkness red and filling the night with lurid, leaping shadows, Ben reached the door into the bunkhouse two steps ahead of Wes. His eyes widened as he saw the thick section of timber that lay across the doorjamb held in position by a rope attached to the door handle to prevent the door from being opened. Ben wasted no time. His knife appeared in his hand and he slashed through the ropes, tossing the section of timber aside and at the same time kicking the door open.

Smoke, like a black ghost, swirled out in a noxious cloud, enveloping and driving him back before it cleared and he lunged inside, eyes smarting. In the glow of the flames he saw the still form of Stumpy huddled on the floor by the table. As he reached the old man the roof at the far end collapsed with a splintering roar.

Ben whirled to see a huge ball of fire, created by the collapsing roof, rushing towards him. His actions were instinctive and lightning fast. He grabbed the table as though it weighed nothing, turned it lengthways across the width of the bunkhouse and dumped it down on its side to form a wall. He hauled Stumpy behind it and ducked down as the ball of fire engulfed it and was deflected over the upper edge and around the sides.

He felt the heat of it wash like the breath of a furnace over him, its passing setting the overhead rafters alight and catching the coverings of the bunks. He had held his breath since entering and his lungs were beginning to protest. He came to his feet, lifted Stumpy, like a baby, into his arms and ran for the open doorway. As he left the bunkhouse the section of roof above the doorway collapsed sending sparks and flame jetting into the air. Sinking to his knees at a safe distance he lowered Stumpy to the earth and drew great, shuddering breaths of cool, night air into his burning lungs.

Angela came rushing across.

'Are you OK, Ben?'

Ben vented a couple of deep coughs and rubbed smoke tears from his eyes.

'I'll be fine, ma'am,' he replied.

'How's Stumpy?'

'He's still alive,' Wes had hunkered down at Stumpy's side and was feeling for life-signs. He looked up. 'Kin you ladies get him back to the house? I need to get this fire under control afore it gets to the barn and the whole place goes up.'

'We can manage,' Angela nodded. 'Come on, Martha.'

For the next two hours the two men hauled buckets of water from the creek, using it to damp down the side of the barn while the bunkhouse burnt itself out. Finally the two were able to drop the wooden buckets and let aching muscles relax. Eyes red-rimmed from smoke and faces red from the heat of the flames the two stood back and let the cool night air take the sting from their tired, aching bodies.

Wes ran a dirty hand through his hair and eyed Ben.

'I figure Clayburn's had his fun. It's about time we started prodding back,' he croaked.

As they headed towards the house neither had given a thought to the women or Stumpy until they entered the house and found Martha. She lay sprawled on the kitchen floor in a pool of blood. Her nose looked to be broken and both swollen cheeks were criss-crossed with deep, straight lacerations.

'She's been pistol-whipped,' Ben said with barely suppressed anger recognizing the marks.

After making Martha comfortable on her bed the two resumed their search for Angela. They found Stumpy tucked up in bed fast asleep, but there was no sign of the redhead.

'What in hell happened here?' Ben demanded.

'Guess we'll have to wait for Martha to come to before we find that out, but I'll allow Clayburn's behind it,' Wes replied wooden-faced. Further speculation was cut short by the sound of hooves outside approaching fast. Wes moved forward and extinguished the lamp while Ben flattened himself against the wall by the window, gun in hand.

'Turning into some night,' he called as Wes arrived to take up position on the other side of the window.

The riders arrived noisily, harness jangling.

'Hey in the house ... step outside.' It was Billy Redland calling.

'What do you want, Redland?' Wes asked.

'You've had a bit of trouble here,' Billy called back.

'Tell me something I don't know,' Wes shouted back. The riders were dark shapes against the glowing red mound of the burnt-out bunkhouse. Easy targets if the two chose to let loose with their guns, but the riders seemed unconcerned.

'Mr Clayburn wants to see you boys,' Billy said. 'Sent us along to make sure you didn't get lost.' His words sparked a general merriment amongst the riders. Ben counted ten in all.

'It gets stranger by the second,' Ben breathed across to Wes.

'Can't figure his game yet, but I'm not too sure I'm about to let Clayburn have his own way.' Wes raised his voice. 'Got a powerful urge to see him myself, but not yet.'

'Wrong, cowboy. Like Billy said, Mr Clayburn wants to see you now.' The words coming from behind were accompanied by the ratchet clicking of bullets being levered into breeches. 'Shuck the guns, boys.' Both recognized the nasal tone of Joe Santos.

While they hesitated a second voice chipped in. It was Smiley.

'We can do this with or without a bullet in yer. I ain't over-bothered which.'

Wes and Ben let their guns drop. Both were angry with themselves for allowing the men to creep up on them. Billy had played the oldest trick, keeping them occupied at the front and allowing Joe and Smiley to get behind. A match scraped and flared and the lamp was lit by a third man.

'Must be getting old,' Ben said disgustedly, tossing Wes an annoyed glance.

'We's got 'em, Billy,' Joe called

'Then bring 'em on out,' Billy called back happily. 'Nice of you boys to join us,' Billy continued as the two emerged. 'Mr Clayburn don't like to be kept waiting.'

Milt Clayburn looked up from his desk as the two were ushered into the room, preceded by a grinning Billy Redland while Joe and Smiley brought up the rear.

'Got 'em, boss,' Billy said unnecessarily as he swaggered to the desk.

'So I see,' Clayburn said coldly. 'Shut the door on your way out.'

Billy's mouth dropped.

'You want us to leave? These two are a mite proddy.'

'Get out, Billy, now,' Clayburn repeated.

'Yes, Billy-boy, get out,' Wes reiterated, earning himself a dark glare from the gunman. Shrugging, Billy left, pushing Joe and Smiley before him. After the door had closed Clayburn eyed the two with amusement in his eyes. The two were dirt-stained and their clothes reeked strongly of smoke from the fire. Smoke grime smeared their faces. Clayburn had removed his coat and the lamplight gleamed on the white, silk sleeves of his shirt.

'Hear you had trouble at the Boxed P tonight?' Clayburn said as he selected a cigar from a box.

'How come I get the feeling that you knew about that before it started?' Ben replied and Clayburn smiled as he lit the cigar. He looked and acted like a man without a care in the world.

'Where's Angela, Clayburn?' Wes asked. 'If anything's happened to her there'll be a funeral at the Circle P; yours.'

'If they find enough of you left to bury,' Ben added with dark menace.

'Very gallant, gentlemen. Now let's cut the bullshit.' Clayburn leaned back in the seat. 'You two are government agents. Like me you are looking for the gold shipment that was stolen a year ago. Unlike me you intend to give it back should you find it. When Frank Parsons and I stole it neither of us planned for one or the other dying before the gold was split up.'

'You admit to the robbery?' Ben asked incredulously.

'Why not? I figure from your presence at the Boxed P you had already worked that out. Telling you is one thing: you proving it is another. The only problem with Frank dying as he did, he took the secret of where he hid the gold with him,' came the surprised answer that had the two staring incredulously at him.

'You mean you don't know where the gold is?' Wes cried as the missing bits of the puzzle fell into place.

'Silly isn't it?' Clayburn laughed. 'But Frank was not supposed to die.'

'How inconsiderate,' Wes murmured. 'You still haven't answered my question. Where's Angela Parsons?'

'Safe ... for the moment, and not on Circle C property. How safe she remains relies on the pair of you.'

'What game are you playing at, Clayburn?' Wes demanded, eyes narrowing.

'It's no game, gentlemen. The fire served two purposes. It showed that I am in deadly earnest and also covered the abduction of Angela Parsons.'

'What about Willy, the kid you ground-dragged behind your horse?' Ben asked quietly.

'A fit of temper, I'm afraid,' Clayburn admitted casually. 'A reprisal for the damage the Boxed P herd did to the grounds fronting the house. The boy was in the wrong place at the wrong time.'

Fury shone in Ben's grey eyes.

'I'll write it on his tombstone,' Ben grated harshly, big hands clenching and unclenching at his sides. Wes saw the danger signs in his friend.

'Say your piece, Clayburn,' Wes broke in quickly. 'You were going to tell us why we are here.'

'I'd have thought that was obvious. You have three days to find the gold and hand it over to me, or the woman dies.'

SEVEN

'I thought you said you didn't play games, Clayburn,' Wes said after a moment's startled silence. 'How the hell are we supposed to do that?'

'A question I have been asking myself ever since Frank died,' Clayburn admitted. 'The answer is that I'll use you two and save myself the trouble.' Clayburn laughed. 'Before you start objecting and refusing, if you fail or refuse, Miss Parsons will die and evidence planted that will implicate both of you. So you see I have the whip hand.'

'Who else was in on the robbery with you and Frank Parsons, Clayburn?' Wes changed the subject. He could see that Ben was getting more agitated by Clayburn's calm, self-assurance, and tried to pacify the situation. Ben had a slow fuse, but when it reached the end the area of the resultant explosion was most definitely not the place to be. Like as not the big man'd take on the entire Circle C single-handed and without a weapon.

'Major Phillips, head of the gold escort troop, was a brief partner, along with two others. Unfortunately he was considered a liability. We four were prepared to wait two years before we touched the gold; he wanted his share straight away.'

'So you dissolved the partnership with a bullet,' Wes sneered.

'It was necessary,' Clayburn agreed calmly and Wes felt a sick, coldness spread through him. Clayburn was insane, devoid of all human feelings and emotions.

'What happened to the bodies?'

'Part of the plan was that I would get rid of the bodies while Frank hid the gold. Part of the Circle C land contains a quicksand. It was easy to dispose of the wagon and bodies in that.'

'You must have trusted Frank a lot to leave him with all that gold?'

'On the contrary. It was because we didn't trust each other that the idea came about.'

Wes frowned. 'How's that again? You left it with a man you didn't trust?'

'Two hundred gold bars, each worth five thousand dollars. Unless you have the right contacts, it's not easy to get rid of stolen gold. Frank had neither the desire or contacts to try.'

'Why the secrecy over its whereabouts?'

'For the same reason. Frank needed me to sell the gold when the time came, but he didn't trust me not to start thinking of ways and means to eliminate him at some time during the waiting period; so he hid the gold and kept the location to himself. You could say it was an agreement of mutual distrust.' Clayburn laughed. 'So the arrangements worked very well until Frank died. Even that did not present too much of a problem to begin with. I had a chance to look for the gold and then she arrived.'

'And you had to get rid of her,' Wes broke in.

'It would have worked. I almost had the Boxed P until you paid her marker,' Clayburn mused darkly, but then his mood lightened. 'Now I don't need it; I have you two to find the gold for me.'

'You keep talking in the singular, Clayburn. What about your other two partners?'

'They died in a fire in town a month after the robbery. Tragic accident,' Clayburn sighed.

'How convenient for you,' Wes sneered and Clayburn smiled.

'Yes, it was,' he agreed, the smile saying the accident was no accident.

'Perhaps I'll break your neck,' Ben rumbled ominously. 'Accidentally.'

'Then the girl will die,' Clayburn said.

'Maybe, maybe not, but you'll never know will you?' Ben took a step forward and the colour drained from Clayburn's face. The look in the big man's eyes told him that Ben was not bluffing.

Clayburn sprang to his feet, the chair crashing over behind him as he clawed his gun from its holster. Wes grabbed Ben's arm.

'Ease up, pard,' he warned.

'With one of you dead it would be harder on the other to do the searching alone,' Clayburn said, heart beating fast as he covered Ben with his gun.

'How do we know she's still alive?' Wes asked.

'Come back in three days and you'll find out,' Clayburn replied viciously.

Dawn was breaking as the two returned to the Boxed P. The band of brightness on the eastern horizon flooded the vast, grass plain with a misty, silver glow.

For Angela Parsons the same dawn was a series of thin, vertical, silver strips. It took a minute, as consciousness returned to identify the silver strips as cracks between wooden boards. She sat up groggily, the action forcing a moan from her dry lips. In the gloomy half-light she saw that she was confined within four, wooden walls of rough, undressed timber. There were no windows in the structure, but she could see a closed door in the wall of silver cracks. The floor beneath her was rock and hard-packed earth so she guessed it was a hut of some sort. The problem was, where? When she moved, chains clanked at her ankles. She sat back against the rear wall, facing the door and staring dully at the ankle chains. Who had done this to her and why?

Her memories were confused. She remembered the fire, Ben saving Stumpy from the burning bunkhouse. She and Martha had carried the unconscious form back to the house leaving Wes and Ben to fight the fire. After laying Stumpy on the bed Martha had gone to the kitchen to fetch water. There had been a scream, the sound of a china bowl breaking followed by an ominous, heavy thud.

Calling Martha's name she had rushed from the bedroom into the darkened hallway. From the open door at the far end, red and black shadows cavorted over the walls;

reflections from the burning bunkhouse. As she prepared to move forward a huge, dark shape rose up before her, so big that it seemed to fill the hallway. Whiskey breath fanned her nostrils. An evil chuckle and…?

There was nothing to follow. She touched the sore place on her chin and winced. Someone had hit her. It must have been one of Clayburn's men, probably Billy Redland. This was another of his tricks. She arose stiffly to her feet and crossed to the door, the chains clanking and chinking at her feet. She tried first pushing then pulling at the handle, but the door refused to budge. A situation that did not surprise her. Next she applied an eye to the largest of the cracks. She had presumed she was somewhere on the Circle C, but the view quickly dispelled that idea.

The sweet smell of pine filled her nostrils. She could see pine trees on either side of a clearing and straight ahead a view of the sun rising between ragged, grey peaks that rose from a sea of thick, white mist. With a shock she realized she was somewhere up in the mountains.

As she continued to look, a figure came into view and a gasp of terror dropped from her lips. She backed away from the crack until the rear wall stopped her, heart thumping in her breast. The figure she had glimpsed was of a man, but a man who only existed in bad dreams and nightmares, not in reality. She pressed herself against the rough timber and listened as heavy, lumbering footsteps pounded nearer and nearer.

Ezra Bodine was big by any standard, a huge mountain of a man. He wore a large, domed ten-gallon hat that appeared small atop his huge, seven-foot frame. The width of his shoulders was less than the girth of his large stomach that bulged through the opening of the front of a red check jacket. Brown cords encased his thick legs with scuffed, leather boots on his feet. Strands of lank, greasy, black hair poked from beneath the hat and clawed down towards small, dark eyes. A dark beard bushed about his lower face. He had so much hair on his face that only a small area below his deep set eyes was clear.

Ezra approached the hut and pulled the wooden block back and pushed the door open. Light flooded over Angela then vanished as Ezra ducked to enter, his hips scraping each side of the doorway. Once inside he rose to his full height, hat almost touching the roof boards, and stared down at her.

'Well good morning, missy,' he rumbled though his beard. 'Ain't it jus' a fine morning?'

'W … who are you and where am I?' She tried to put authority in her voice and failed. It came out as a high-pitched squeak.

Ezra stroked his beard with a huge hand. 'Ain't that a question though?' he replied. 'Why you're our guest, missy.' He brayed an unpleasant laugh.

'Our?' Angela felt herself quaking inside.

'Me and my baby brother Jubal. I'm Ezra

and we's the Bodines.' His eyes raked the curves of her body hotly as he spoke. 'As to where you'm be.' He eyed her, hands on hips. 'Here!' he rattled out and broke into another bout of gruff laughter. 'Here. Do you get it, missy? Here.'

'Baby' brother Jubal, as she later found out, was the image of Ezra and perhaps a shade taller, but minus the beard.

'How did I get here?'

'We brunged you, Jubal and me.' His eyes settled on the swell of her breasts and a pink tongue darted about his bearded lips. She felt her fear increase as, unconsciously, she brought a hand to her breasts. The movement brought a flicker of amusement to Ezra's eyes.

'Who paid you to do this? Was it Milt Clayburn?' she demanded.

'My, don' you ask a lotta questions? Fair makes a body's head spin. Seems to me that's the gent's name.' He nodded.

'Well I'll double whatever he gave you to let me go.'

'Can't rightly do that,' he said after a pause. 'You gotta stay and look after Jubal and me.'

Angela clutched at her throat as panic spread through her.

'What do you mean?' Her voice was barely above a whisper.

'He said you'd like that and jus' now we're powerful hungry. We kin fun later. Said you liked to fun.' A sly look came in his eyes. 'Maybe you'd like to fun now, eh, missy?' He leered at her and leaned forward. Hot, foul, whiskey-tainted breath washed over her face making her stomach heave. She turned her head away, closing her eyes.

'Hey, Ezra, where you at? I'm getting plumb starved to nothing!' A voice from outside turned Ezra back with a scowl and for the moment she breathed a sigh of relief.

'Ain't but one body it could have been and there's two of 'em,' Stumpy said with a shake of his head. 'The Bodines, Ezra and Jubal.'

When Wes and Ben had returned to the Boxed P, they found both Martha and Stumpy up. Martha's battered cheeks and broken nose were of some concern to the boys, but she waved aside the suggestion of a doctor. Though her face and nose were badly swollen she managed a painful smile.

'Ain't much he could for this ol' face. I'll make out. It's Miss Angie I'm concerned for. That poor chile ain't gonna know what's a-happening.'

Stumpy, suffering more from a hangover than the injury he had received falling, could remember little of the previous evening. He had heard nothing of the attack on the two women, but from Martha's description of her attacker had no trouble identifying him.

'Are you sure, Stumpy?' Wes asked.

'Ain't nobody as big as those boys in the whole territory and that's for sure,' Stumpy asserted. 'If'n the fella that attacked you didn't have no chin whiskers, that was Jubal. They gotta cabin up in the mountains and work hauling logs for the sawmill in Freedom. Seen 'em in town on occasion. Spend their money on whiskey, lotsa whiskey. One thing's for sure. The Bodines are mean folk. No one gets in their way. No, sirree!' Stumpy was adamant.

'Then we best get Miss Angie back. Figure Clayburn paid those fellas to take her, figuring again that we wouldn't know who it was,' Ben said. 'How do we find these Bodines?'

'T'ain't difficult. Pick up the old Trapper's Trail ten miles north-east of here and follow that up into the mountains. That trail leads plumb straight into their place.' He scowled at the two. 'Only they don't take kindly to strangers.'

'That's OK, Stumpy, we don't aim to be kind strangers,' Wes remarked.

'Well you boys haul off and get yourselves cleaned up. Get some good food inside you before you go charging off,' Martha butted in with an expression that dared them to argue. 'You look like scarecrows or worse.'

Wes and Ben eyed each other.

'Guess you're right, Martha,' Ben admitted with a wry smile.

Less than an hour later, cleaned and fed and wearing the same garb Stumpy had first seen them in, the two set out. Before they left Stumpy drew them aside.

'Didn't want to make too much of it in front of Martha, but them Bodines, they don't have much respect for womenfolk. Stories I heard tell...' He shuddered at the mere thought of them. 'They're animals, if'n you get my drift?'

'Loud and clear, Stumpy,' Wes replied looking grim. 'How long to their place?'

'Three, mebbe four hours. Just remember they'd as soon kill you as shake hands.'

'Not feeling too friendly myself at the moment,' Ben pointed out, stoney-faced.

At first it seemed that the two immense brothers were content for her to cook and clean for them; that Ezra's clumsy seduction attempt was a one-off, heat-of-the-moment affair, but that idea rapidly changed. Breakfast over, Ezra Bodine had left the cabin. She was glad to see the big, bearded form vanish from sight. She had felt his hot, piggy eyes burning into her back as she washed the pans and dishes. But her relief was short-lived as the beardless Jubal backed her into a corner minutes later.

'How 'bout you be good to Jubal, girl?' He leered down at her, grinning through yellow, tobacco-stained teeth. Dark, unkempt hair hung about his face. He gripped her shoulders in his huge hands.

'You're hurting me!' she gasped, throwing ineffectual blows at his chest, fear drying her mouth as once again her heart began to beat in distress.

'T'ain't nuthin', but a little hug,' he protested and lowered his head in an effort to kiss her, but she snapped her head to one side. First Ezra in the hut, now Jubal. 'C'mon, girl, a little kiss for Jubal. Show a body how you like him,' Jubal coaxed as she struggled to free herself. The strong, acrid odour of sweat and unwashed clothes clawed into her nostrils.

Cursing, Jubal released a hand to grab her chin and hold her head steady. As his face descended again, she butted forward and rammed her forehead hard against his lips.

Jubal gave a cry and released her, staggering back a half step, blood oozing from a mashed, lower lip. He wiped the blood away with the back of a grimy hand and stared first at the red smear before letting his hate-filled gaze settle on her. The look in his eyes chilled her to the marrow.

'Keep away from me!' she shrilled.

'Ain't but one way to tame a hell-cat like you, girl,' he breathed, 'But we's got work to do, the funning comes later.' He grabbed a handful of her hair and dragged her brutally from the cabin towards the hut. Ezra looked up from honing an axe.

'What's the matter, boy? She too much for you?' he jeered.

Later, locked once again in the hut, she sank to the earth floor and the tears flooded out.

The trail led up through the tall pines, affording cool, welcome shade after the sun of the plains. Occasionally, to the left, the trees would thin enough to give them dramatic views of deep, sweeping valleys and tall, eagle-haunted crags. They rode in single file, Wes in the lead. They had ridden hard to reach the Trapper's Trail and hoped to cut Stumpy's estimated time by half. Now, they let the horses do the leading at their own pace on the steep, rising trail.

They had reached a point where the trail levelled temporarily before another steep ascent, when Wes reined to a halt, staring up and ahead. As Ben edged alongside he raised a finger.

'Up ahead,' Wes said softly.

At the top of the next ascent Ben could make out the roof angles of a log cabin.

'Home, sweet home,' Ben breathed with a taut smile.

They dismounted and tethered their horses off the trail before advancing on foot and crouching just below the top of the rise to take a cautious look around. The cabin was set on a flat plateau ringed with pines. On the far side of the cabin lay a small corral where a pair of horses grazed contentedly. These were the only signs of life visible. So it proved minutes later after the two had stolen to the cabin only to find it empty. Standing outside the cabin, Wes cocked an ear, the gun he had palmed earlier now back in its holster.

Apart from the birdsong, the surrounding trees were silent.

'It's too damn quiet,' Wes said.

'Maybe this is the wrong place?' Ben suggested to hide his disappointment.

'Let's take a look around,' Wes replied.

They came upon the small, windowless hut a few minutes later. It stood in a small clearing a hundred yards from the cabin. Ringed by trees, a pile of logs, ready for transporting to Freedom, were piled a few yards to the right of the hut. Wes drew his Colt as he crossed to the door of the hut, indicating the crude wooden block that acted as a bolt, with a nod of his head to Ben.

'Sure would stop a person getting out,' Ben said. Wes rapped on the door with the barrel of his gun.

'Anyone at home?' he called.

Inside, Angela's head snapped up in wonderment. Scrambling to her feet she wondered if her ears were playing a cruel trick on her.

'Wes?'

Outside Wes threw Ben a triumphant look. 'Looks like we just hit the jackpot, big fella. Hold on, Miss Angie. We'll have you out of there in no time.' Wes could not believe their luck. To get in and out of the Bodines' camp, rescue the girl and get away without tangling with the legendary Bodines, seemed too good to be true.

It was!

EIGHT

Jubal Bodine stood behind the hut, a long-handled axe gripped in his hands, the sweat of anticipation beading his face. Ezra had positioned himself behind the pile of logs. A cruel smile beamed across his bearded face as he threw a look at the two by the door and flexed his arms.

The rumble of logs caused both men to snap their heads around in time to see the top section of the log pile collapse and begin to roll and bounce towards them. Ben darted sideways trying to get around the side of the hut only to find himself running on to the head of the axe that Jubal used in lance fashion. The blow doubled him over until the grinning Jubal used the handle to side swing at Ben's jaw.

Ben straightened, spun and slammed face

forward against the side of the hut, the Adams spinning from his hand. As he came dazedly from the wall, Jubal came from behind and used the handle of the axe, under Ben's chin, to form a crushing bar across his throat.

'I got me this one, Ezra,' Jubal crowed with delight as he hauled back on the axe, cutting off Ben's breathing.

Wes had fared even worse. The first log had hit the corner of the hut and swung inwards in a scything sweep across the front of the hut. Wes had seen Jubal butt the axe-head into Ben's midriff and was levelling his Colt to blow Jubal's head off when the log rammed his legs and drove him face first against the wooden wall. The gun flew from his grip as he was driven to his knees. More logs followed the first as he went to his knees, pinning his legs.

Ezra came pounding up, whooping joyfully as the avalanche of logs came to halt. Wes was face to the front of the hut and trying to rise when Ezra grabbed the back of his head and slammed his face hard against the wooden wall and with a moan Wes toppled sideways.

'Got me one too, brother,' Ezra sang out gleefully.

Inside the hut, Angela pounded on the door.

'What's happening?' she shouted.

'Ain't nuthin' to worry about, missy, jus' a coupla' gents on the prowl, but we's took care of them,' Ezra called back.

Ben had managed to get his hands on to the axe handle and was pushing against Jubal's pull. He had managed to ease the pressure.

'Sure is a lively one,' Jubal gasped as Ben twisted and jerked against his body.

'Best give you some help, boy, afore he wriggles plumb clear,' Ezra said as he lumbered forward.

Ben's forearms were aching under the strain of pushing the handle from his throat. Already weakened from the earlier blows he knew it would only be a matter of time before the handle crushed the life from his body.

'Ain't needing no help with this tiddler,' Jubal grunted, sweat pouring down his face now, affronted that Ezra should suggest he needed help.

Ezra came forward and halted, a grin on his bearded features, but it was a grin that vanished behind a startled yelp. With only his toes on the ground as Jubal arched backwards, Ben brought a foot up in a high kick that caught Ezra full on the chin, staggered him back and dropped him on to his ample backside. Next, Ben stamped down on to the instep of Jubal's right foot and then left foot; Jubal let out a howl and his grip loosened enough for Ben to push the handle away and duck clear.

Agony creased Jubal's sweating face as Ben went down on one knee, drawing air into his lungs. Ben could see Ezra scrambling to his feet. He hoisted up as with a roar Jubal forgot his hurts and lurched forward, swinging the axe. Had it connected Ben would have been minus his head. As it was Ben leapt backwards colliding with the side of the hut as the axe head buried itself deep in the wood by his head.

Ben came away from the wall, grim determination setting his features hard. He slammed a fist into Jubal's stomach, feeling it sink to the wrist before fat and muscle bounced it out. A normal human being would have been floored by the blow. Jubal emitted a gasp of air, but remained standing. Ben changed tactics and stamped his foot against the side of Jubal's right knee. This had the desired effect. Jubal's leg collapsed under him and he toppled sideways clawing air and howling. His fall impeded Ezra's angry advance and Ben took the opportunity to make a break while he could still stand. He leapt aside and ran towards the trees.

If he was hoping to gain a little respite to reorganize and rethink his next move, he was sadly disappointed. Ezra cussed Jubal as he hauled him up and both came lumbering after him. Ben pressed forward into a deepening, green gloom, heart thudding and jumping in his chest. He was angry with himself for being lulled into a false sense of security. The Bodines had taken Wes and himself by complete surprise. In fact it seemed to him that everyone was taking them by surprise on this job.

The gloom lifted about him as he emerged into an area of dense oak and brush. Behind him he could hear the Bodines. Big as they were they could certainly move or maybe he was moving slower than he thought.

Patches of blue grew larger overhead as the leaf canopy grew less. He burst through a screen of leaves and the trees vanished. He saw soaring peaks ahead and fearsome, grey-faced crags. Unfortunately as the trees vanished so did the ground. He teetered on the edge of a sheer drop that fell to jumbled rocks five hundred feet below. Sweat exploded over his body as impetus drove him forward. He windmilled his arms and arched back in an effort to save himself, but all to no avail. With a wild cry he tumbled forward. One hand grabbed on to an oak branch that overhung the drop and he held on for dear life.

The branch creaked but held. He grabbed on with his other hand and swung gently, three feet out from the cliff face. It was as he hung there that Jubal appeared on the edge above him amid the greenery. A grin spread across Jubal's face as he saw Ben.

'Well lookee here! Hey, Ezra, you seen this boy?'

'I see him, Jubal.' Ezra joined his grinning brother. 'I declare that that boy must be the luckiest son alive. Ain't but one place he coulda grabbed a branch, but here.'

Ben gritted his teeth. His heart was in his throat.

'Are you going to help me?' he called.

'Help you fly, mebbe,' Jubal replied. 'But I reckon you're wrong about him being lucky, brother.'

'How come?' Ezra demanded.

Jubal lifted his axe.

'Cause I'm gonna cut that ol' branch off.' Jubal giggled and Ezra joined in with his deeper chuckles.

'That'll be murder,' Ben shouted back, panic fluttering in his stomach.

'Yep!' Jubal agreed. 'Seems you could be right, but ain't no one about to say one way or t'other.' With that he raised the axe and brought it down with a solid thud on to the branch. Ben felt the shock of the blow shiver the length of the branch.

'You can't do this, Bodine,' Ben shouted.

The axe-head flashed again. This time the keen-edged blade sheared through the branch and Ben felt himself drop, still clinging uselessly to the severed branch.

On the top of the cliff Jubal smiled to himself.

'I jus' did,' he said.

When Wes came to he found himself staring up at the blue sky wondering why he could not move his arms or legs. It was only by craning his aching head left and right that he found himself spreadeagled on the ground, fastened by ropes to four stakes driven into the ground before the cabin. The action of moving his head sent steel lances biting into his brain forcing an involuntary groan from his lips. The sound brought Jubal into his line of vision. He stared up at the fat, grinning face.

'I wus wondering when you were gonna wake up, boy,' Jubal said casually. 'Don' have visitors overmuch, so wouldn't want you to miss out on the entertainment.' He chuckled. 'Specially as you's it!' He laughed again, belly jerking in spasms. 'Hey, Ezra, he's awake.'

Wes turned his head as the bearded Ezra approached from the other direction.

'Where's Ben?' Wes croaked up at him.

'You meaning that boy with the silver hair?'

'Where is he?'

'Bottom of Eagle Ridge if'n I ain't missing my guess,' Ezra replied. 'What do you say, Jubal?'

'That's the way he was heading last time I

see'd him.' The giggle exploded from his lips. 'From the top. The boy thought he could fly so we'uns obliged.'

Wes felt a sick anger build up inside him.

'Thought I heard him change his mind halfway down,' Ezra joked. 'But then it was too late.' Ezra's grin faded. 'Why did you and your friend come here sneaking around? What were you looking for?'

'You figure it out,' Wes shot back and received a boot in the ribs for his trouble.

'Figure you were looking for the girl,' he said. 'Who sent you, boy?'

'Just followed the smell you left,' Wes said recklessly and Jubal supplied the kick from the other side.

'It don' do to get too sassy,' Ezra pointed out. 'It don' make no matter who sent you, they ain't gonna get much back. Found your horses down the trail apiece. Reckon they belong to us now.'

'You won't get away with this, Bodine. Someone will come looking for the girl or us,' Wes bluffed.

'Is that a fact?' Ezra sneered. 'We'll have to make sure they don' find you then. Bring the girl here, Jubal.'

A few minutes later Jubal returned with Angela. When she saw Wes staked out she broke free of Jubal's loose grip and ran, chains clanking, to Wes's side and dropped to her knees. Sorrow charged her eyes as she looked at his battered, bloodstained face.

'Oh, Wes.' The words fell brokenly from her lips.

Wes forced a painful smile.

'We'll have to stop meeting like this,' he joked as tears welled in her eyes.

'I'm sorry, Wes.'

'Nothing to be sorry about, ma'am. Hazards of the job. Have they hurt you?'

'No.' She cast her eyes about. 'Ben?' Her eyes settled on his face.

'Seems like the big fella ran out of luck this time,' he said quietly.

Angela's fists balled and her head dropped.

'Don' they make a fine couple?' Jubal jeered.

'Gets yer plumb in the heart.'

'Gets me plumb in the stomach,' Ezra replied sourly. 'Makes a body feel real hungry.' He grabbed her brutally by the hair and hauled her to her feet causing her to cry out in agony. 'Time you were cooking, missy.'

Wes struggled futilely against his bonds, anger suffusing his face.

'Don't hurt her, Bodine!' he yelled.

Ezra's face broke into a nasty grin.

'What are you gonna do 'bout it, boy?'

'Reckon he can't do nuthin', Ezra,' Jubal sang out. 'Reckon he'd like to though.'

'Let's eat and think on how best to deal with this boy.' Ezra, dragging Angela with a chuckling Jubal in tow, headed for the cabin.

Wes closed his eyes and thought, 'Dammit, Ben. Why'd you pick this moment to die...?'

The moment for Ben to die had not yet arrived. Had the Bodines taken the trouble to look over the edge after he had fallen, they would have seen him, thirty feet down, clinging to a ledge of rock no more than an inch wide with torn, bloodstained fingers. When the branch had been cut it had swung him against the cliff face. Releasing his grip of the severed limb he had reached out with clawing fingers at the unyielding rock as it flew by. Skin and nails were ripped from his fingertips, but fear deadened the pain. He had automatically locked his fingers when he had felt the edge of the ledge against his wrists and the next second he found himself hanging against the face of the cliff like a giant spider.

To Ben that moment seemed like hours ago. He had no idea how long he had hung there, but when the realization hit him that he was not dead, he began to think about how to get out of the situation he was in. As Wes was being staked out by the Bodines, Ben began the slow, tortuous climb back to the top.

Sweat poured down his face and soaked dark patches beneath his armpits. After finding toe holds he had studied the rock face above his head. Some twenty feet up a thick root section of a tree bulged like a handle from a crevice in the rock. Cracks at all angles covered the rock face between him and the root. There was nothing wide enough for him to get his fingers into and it seemed as though his fate was about to take a turn for the worst when an idea came.

Wes had just received his first kick from Ezra when Ben, holding on with one hand, drew his knife with another. He then jammed the blade of the knife into the widest crack and to his surprise it held. Using the knife, the ledge that he had clung to earlier he now stood on and the loop of tree root looked a lot closer, but there was still a ways to go. He rested for a moment. A cool breeze fanned his heated face and gave the sweat beads an icy feel. Also now, his lacerated fingertips were beginning to throb with pain. He gritted his teeth and worked the knife free from a crack. Each move he made with exaggerated slowness. He knew that any jerky movement could tumble him to the rocks below.

The knife blade scratched the rock as he slid it towards the next crack.

'Well, boy, we reckon we'uns have come up with the perfect idea,' Ezra boasted as later, fed and liquored, he and Jubal returned to Wes. 'You and Jubal are gonna fight for the girl.' He grinned down at Wes. Angela, who was being held by Jubal, gave a shocked gasp.

'What happens if I win?' Wes asked, a question that caused the brothers a good deal of laughter.

'This boy sure is a load of laughs,' Ezra wheezed. 'Why, if'n you win you take the girl here and git.'

'Well let's get on with it,' Wes snapped.

'He sure is anxious to die,' Jubal observed happily.

'Wes, you can't,' Angela objected. 'He'll kill you.'

'Seems he's gonna do that anyway,' Wes observed calmly.

Ezra drew a knife and slashed the ropes holding Wes down.

'If'n you got ideas of making a run for it, remember we still got the girl.'

Wes climbed stiffly to his feet, pulling the ropes from his wrists. He heard Angela scream his name and looked up in time to see a fist, the size of a ham, heading towards him. It caught West on the side of the chin, lifted him off his feet and laid him down on his back with a slam that knocked the breath from his body.

With a roar Jubal launched himself towards Wes who was struggling weakly to rise. Jubal helped him, hauling him to his feet by his shirt-front. Wes's head was still spinning. He slammed two punches into Jubal's stomach and for all the effect it had he may as well not have bothered.

Jubal slapped him back and forth across the face with an open hand, grinning all the time. Wes threw another couple of ineffectual punches before Jubal tossed him aside contemptuously.

'This is too easy,' he moaned across to Ezra.

Ezra stood behind Angela, gripping her shoulders, forcing her to watch.

Wes launched himself headfirst in a butt to Jubal's stomach. He bounced off and Jubal laughed. Jubal hauled him up again and flung his arms around Wes, trapping the man's arms at his side, then lifting him off his feet he began to squeeze.

For Wes it was like being caught in a huge press. Jubal's arms were like iron bands about him, slowly squeezing the life from his body. Wes was helplessly trapped. As a roaring filled his head he knew that he would need a miracle to survive this.

From a long way off he heard Angela screaming for Jubal to stop. It was mixed with the sound of his own bones creaking under the awful pressure. He was going to die and there was nothing he could do to save himself.

NINE

Wes wanted to scream his agony, but his lungs were empty and the arms about his body prevented him from breathing more in. A roaring filled his head, the sound reminding him of a waterfall plunging into a deep, deep abyss. Then, just as he thought that his creaking ribs could take no more, Jubal gave a jerk and a grunt. If Wes had had his eyes open he would have seen Jubal's eyes widen in shocked disbelief. Wes felt the crushing grip slacken, felt himself sliding down against Jubal's quivering body. His feet touched the ground, but his legs refused to take his weight and he crashed to the ground sucking in great lungfuls of pine-flavoured air. His eyes flickered open and he managed to lever himself up on elbows. Jubal stood before him, a dazed, disbelieving expression slackening the muscles of his face.

Ezra stared across at his brother.

'Quit your fooling, Jubal,' he shouted.

In reply Jubal tried to reach his hands behind his back. The effort caused him to turn around and it was Wes's turn to look surprised. The bone handle of a knife was buried to the hilt between his shoulder blades.

Ezra saw it at the same moment and let out a startled roar and pushed the girl from him. Jubal sank to his knees and after giving Ezra a final, pleading look, fell forward on his face and lay still. Wes recognized the knife, but didn't dare believe it until Ben stepped clear of the trees and strode purposefully towards Ezra. Ezra could only stand and stare with slack-jawed wonder at the approaching figure.

'It ain't possible,' he breathed.

'Maybe I did learn to fly,' Ben said grimly, eyes, ice chips in a granite-set face.

'What took you so long?' Wes croaked.

'Are you complaining?' Ben asked, his eyes

never leaving Ezra's bearded face.

'Not yet, but give me time,' Wes responded with a half smile.

To give Ezra his due, he recovered quickly from the shock and a vicious smile tugged at his bearded lips.

'Knowed I shoulda took you m'sel',' he rumbled. He wore no gun, but a wicked looking knife appeared in his hand as he launched himself to meet Ben.

Ben made no move to avoid the charging Ezra even though he weighed a good hundred pounds more than he. Ben was sore. He needed a physical release of the anger and frustration that had built up within him. Ezra struck down with the knife and Ben caught the descending wrist in his left hand and drove his right into Ezra's stomach. The blow hurt Ezra and for the first time in his life a feeling of uncertainty rose within him. He had never met another man who could match his strength; hurt him. It was a unique experience and one he didn't like. Even Jubal had never beaten him in a display of strength.

He jerked free of Ben's grip, lips pursed and staggered back, surprise in his eyes as he looked at Ben. He rubbed a hand over his stomach.

'I'm gonna enjoy killing you, boy,' he bragged and smiled darkly, but tone and expression reflected the doubt that had sprung into his mind.

As the two circled each other, Wes took the opportunity to crawl out of the way and Angela helped him to his feet.

Ezra moved in on Ben again, his sour body odour filling the silver-haired man's flaring nostrils. Ezra threw a punch at Ben's head that Ben blocked easily, but the punch was a cover to hide the upward, scything movement of the knife. Still blocking the arm, Ben turned sideways and deflected the knife hand with his left wrist. At the same moment he clenched the fingers of his right hand that still held Ezra's left arm at bay and unloaded a punch to the jaw that had Ezra reeling back, looking for the boulder that had hit him. All of Ben's anger and frustration was in that blow. It would have taken an ordinary man's head off and slammed it into the next county, but Ezra Bodine was no ordinary man. Even so it had its effect. Ezra had never been floored by a punch before, but this one turned him around and sent him sprawling, facing away from Ben. With surprising agility Ezra scrambled around and straightened, on his knees before Ben, the knife still clutched in his hand. Ben lashed out with a foot. It caught the knife-clenched fist and Ezra let out a yell of pain as his hand was kicked sideways and mashed, stinging fingers released the knife.

Ezra lurched to his feet and came at Ben again, arms open wide to apply the same deadly hug that Jubal had used on Wes, howling to intimidate his opponent. It had no effect on Ben. He stood his ground and Ezra felt as though he had walked into the side of a mountain. Ezra's talents lay in brute strength. He had never learned the finer points of fist-fighting. Ben's punching was precise and devastating. It stopped Ezra in his tracks, driving the breath from his body and snapping his head from side to side. Ben would have finished him then and there, but the fickle nature of fate decided to play its trump card.

As he moved in on Ezra, Angela clapped her hands to her mouth and screamed, eyes wide.

'Ben, watch out!' Wes shouted hoarsely. Even Ezra's eyes registered disbelief as something moved behind Ben.

Ben caught movement in the corner of one eye and the next second a thick, crushing arm from behind wrapped itself about his throat and harsh, gurgling breathing sounded in his ear and Jubal said, 'You're dead meat, cowboy!'

They had all thought that Jubal was dead, but some inner spark refused to let the man die quickly. Driven by some dark, inner force, he had risen up. His chin and shirt front were stained bright red with blood that ran from his mouth. Using just one arm he pulled Ben back against his bloodstained body.

Ben jabbed an elbow back into the man's stomach. Once, twice and on the third attempt Jubal began to weaken, bending forward as Ben's blows took effect, his hold relaxing a little. Gripping the arm, Ben pivoted forward jamming his rear into Jubal's midriff.

In a show of strength that surprised Ezra, Jubal's feet left the ground as Ben lifted four hundred pounds on his back, then tilted his left shoulder down. Jubal slid sideways, the arm at Ben's throat straightening and he crashed down on his back, pushing the knife even deeper into his flesh. The effort sent Ben, scarlet faced, to his knees. Jubal's legs kicked convulsively, then the light of life fled from his eyes and his harsh, laboured breathing stopped as the death he had shouldered aside claimed him.

The heart gone out of him, Ezra turned and ran. He lashed out at Wes and sent the weakened man sprawling. Next, he closed on Angela and swung a second blow that almost snapped the head from her shoulders. He needed an edge over the silver-haired cowboy and she would provide it. As she sagged he hoisted her over his left shoulder as though she weighed nothing and in a lumbering run made for the trees.

Ben shook the dizziness from his head and came to his feet. For all his size Ezra moved quickly. Ben looked up in time to see Ezra vanishing into the trees with his burden and started in pursuit. Wes, after picking himself up, ran to where their horses had been tied. His revolver lay somewhere in the vicinity of the hut. The Winchester in the saddle scabbard lay closer. He hauled it clear and followed the direction Ben had taken.

Ezra moved quickly through the trees, twisting this way and that as he followed barely visible, animal trails, his confidence slowly returning as the deep, green gloom enveloped him. The forest and mountains were his domain and he knew both like the back of his hand. He knew that his progress was noisy, but sounds become deceptive in the forest, direction distorted. This was something that Ben knew and minutes later came to a halt, listening. Sweat sheened his face and pasted strands of silver hair to his forehead. He heard a distant crashing some way ahead and to the left.

Wes arrived at his side.

'Which way?' he croaked.

'Somewhere up there,' Ben replied negatively. Without sighting his quarry it would be very easy to miss the path Ezra had taken with Angela. Ben searched for signs in the carpet of pine needles, picking out areas of disturbance before finally leading off.

The gloom lightened as they came into an area of oak and brush. They had been steadily climbing and the ground beneath became more and more stony and scattered with moss-backed rocks. By the time they broke clear of the trees, both men were gasping for breath, their clothing soaked in sweat. Wes leant back against a tree and dragged air into his lungs while Ben hunkered down to stare at the ground.

Ahead rose a great buttress of rock that stubbed a flattened head into a blue sky splashed with a few wispy puffs of white cloud.

'That boy sure can move,' Wes gasped out as he slowly recovered his breath, and waited for Ben to indicate their direction. Ben was a superb tracker and even on this hard, unyielding terrain, he should be able to pick up sign.

Ben arose and cast about looking for a stone that had been turned, moss crushed. Steep scree slopes lay at the base of the buttress. Ben indicated ahead, in a direction flanking the scree slopes with the curve of the forest to the right. At first the way was clear, but very soon they entered a patch of oak and thorny scrub and Ben found fragments of cloth and threads caught on the thorns. Heartened, he increased his pace. The path struck inwards, climbing steeply and as they emerged within the shadow of the buttress a choked off scream filled their ears.

'Bodine!' Ben's voice crashed through the stillness. Close to a cavemouth Ezra Bodine was grappling with a conscious Angela. Ezra jumped at the sound of Ben's voice and drew Angela before him. Wrapping an arm about her neck he placed the flat of his other hand against the side of her head.

'Keep back, boy, or I'll break her neck,' Ezra shouted, eyes flicking from one to the other.

'It's over, Bodine. Let her go!' Ben called as he motioned Wes to a standstill.

'Can't do that,' Ezra shouted back. 'While I got this little missy, you gotta do as I say, if'n you wanna keep her alive. Now shuck that gun, boy,' he directed at Wes.

'If she dies so do you, Bodine, the hard way,' Ben promised.

'Listen to Ben here. He knows a whole heap of ways of killing a man real slow like,' Wes said.

'Maybe so, but it ain't gonna do missy here any good. The gun, get rid of it, slide it across to me and real gentle like,' Ezra purred.

'No!' Ben barked as Wes prepared to do Ezra's bidding and brought surprised stares from all three. 'Not this time, Ezra Bodine. With that rifle in your hands you'll as like kill us as look at us, the lady included.'

'Mebbe so,' Ezra agreed, 'but you ain't got no choice. I'll kill her now less'en you pass that rifle across.' To back his words, Ezra forced Angela's head sideways until her face became a mask of agony and mewling cries of pain dropped from her lips.

'Then you'll die straight after,' Ben shouted desperately. 'Seems to me that a smart man would want to stay alive?'

'How's that again, boy?'

'Ease up on her, Bodine. There's a way we can all walk away from this.' Ben was sweating for Angela's sake.

'If'n you're trying to trick ol' Ezra?' The warning was not lost in his voice, but he relaxed the pressure on Angela's head and Ben breathed easy again. He was playing a desperate game with high stakes and the odds were not in his favour.

'No tricks,' Ben promised. 'I'm not interested in killing you. I only want the girl. Let her go and you can walk away from here. That way we all stay alive and everyone's happy.'

Ezra scowled.

'Jubal ain't happy. He's dead,' he pointed out sourly.

'I take you for a smart man, Ezra in as much as you don't want to end up like your brother.'

Ezra appeared thoughtful.

'You trying to jaw the man to death?' Wes whispered from the corner of his mouth and before Ben could frame a suitable reply, Ezra's voice rasped across the clearing.

'Ain't got much chance agin the rifle yo' friend carries.'

'Toss it behind you, Wes,' Ben ordered.

Wes eyed the stone profile of his friend, seemed ready to argue, thought better of it and threw the rifle down behind him.

'It's gone, Ezra,' Wes called.

'You boys move on down the trail apiece and then I'll let her go.'

'No deal!' Ben said coldly.

'Then mebbe I'll break her neck and take my chances,' Ezra breathed and Ben felt his blood run cold. He could reach the two in a few seconds, but Ezra could snap her neck in half the time.

'Bodine ... NO...!' Ben shouted and started forward only to stop again as his shout got tangled with a snarl as something dark and bulky broke low from the bushes to Ezra's right. Ezra's head snapped around and a look of terror filled his eyes as a black coated grizzly rose on its stumpy hind legs and the snarl became a deep-throated roar from the gaping muzzle.

With a yell of terror, Ezra pushed Angela into the path of the lumbering beast. Angela screamed as Wes and Ben looked on helplessly. It was the chains, hobbling her legs that saved her life. Unable to move her feet with the impetus of the shove, she stumbled and fell. As she hit the ground, jarring knees and wrists she had the presence of mind to throw herself to one side. The grizzly, towering a good ten feet into the air, ignored her and charged, front paws waving, straight at Ezra. The huge man seemed unable to move until a set of curving claws raked the flesh from his right cheek and tore his ear away in the process.

Ezra screamed and staggered back towards the cave entrance. This seemed to enrage the grizzly even more. Its roars mingled with Ezra's hoarse screams as the man threw punches at the beast's chest. Ben ran to Angela and scooped up the shocked girl.

The arms of the grizzly closed about Ezra in a crushing grip. The man managed to keep one arm free and tried to ward off the beast's snapping jaws. There was a sickening crunch. The grizzly shook its head and Ezra's hand flew from its bloodstained mouth.

'Help me!' Ezra screamed as blood fountained from the severed wrist and soaked into the grizzly's dark fur. Angela buried her head in Ben's chest, her body shaking.

Wes, in the meantime, was hunting his rifle that he had tossed away. It had slithered beneath a thorn bush and by the time he had retrieved it, it was too late to help Ezra. The man was dead, part of his face chewed away by the powerful jaws of the grizzly, head lolling as he hung limply in its grasp. As the grizzly dropped the still form Wes raised the Winchester, but Ben stayed his arm.

'Can't save him now, look!' Two cubs had appeared at the mouth of the cave. 'Guess she was only protecting her own.' He turned away and the others followed.

They returned to the cabin where Ben struck the leg irons from Angela's legs while Wes collected their revolvers and Ben's knife. Later, Ben saddled a horse from the Bodines' corral for Angela and the three returned down the Trapper's Trail, glad to get off the mountain with its death and dark memories.

It was dark by the time the three reached the Boxed P to a joyful reunion from Martha and Stumpy. On the journey back they had told Angela how they had traced her from Stumpy's identification of Martha's description of her attacker.

'All we gotta do now is find the gold and settle with Clayburn,' Wes said casually as though it was the easiest thing in the world. They were gathered in the lounge of the house, each with a glass of Stumpy's fine 'sipping' whiskey. Wes had told Martha and Stumpy about the gold, seeing no reason to keep it a secret from them any longer.

'And how do you propose to do that?' Angela asked.

'I reckon these boys can do whatever they've a mind too,' Stumpy opined, still marvelling over the tale of the day's events on the mountain.

'We try, Stumpy,' Ben said with a grin. 'And now it's our turn to hold the ace card. Clayburn will not know that Miss Angie is safe. Reckon we should keep that bit of knowledge to ourselves. Make him think he still has the edge. Means you'll have to stay in the house during the day and keep out of sight, ma'am.' He looked at Angela who nodded her agreement. 'Give us time to think of our next move,' Ben ended.

'And that is?' Angela asked.

'Sleep, ma'am.' Ben grinned. 'I'm just about all in.'

TEN

Otis Mason scratched at his bony, hatchet nose, brow furrowed in thought. In his early sixties, he still boasted a full head of hair, albeit white. A thin, cadaverous individual, faintly resembling the clucking, pecking chickens he kept.

'What sort o' fella was Frank Parsons?' Otis repeated Ben's question in a musing way.

It had been Stumpy's idea that they pay a visit to Otis Mason who ran a small, chicken farm, five miles south of Freedom.

'Stumpy said that if any man knew Frank it would be you,' Wes prompted. 'You worked for him for a spell.' Wes sat in a hard-backed chair on the veranda of Otis's house facing Otis, whose bony frame was bent into a creaking rocker. Ben, with nowhere else to sit, perched himself on the veranda rail between the two. House was rather a grand name for the structure that squatted in the shade of a cotton-wood stand. It looked like a converted cowshed. All around, hundreds of chickens scratched in the dust and filled the air with their incessant clucking.

'Reckon I did know Frank better'n most,' Otis nodded as he fetched an ancient corn-cob pipe into view. 'And you know what?' He squinted from one to the other and gave neither a chance to answer. 'He was the meanest, tight-fisted cuss for many a mile.' Otis nodded again and lit his pipe. 'Never had no regular crew at the Boxed P. Too mean for that. Used to hire men for round-up and then fire 'em when it was done. Most time he was on his own at that place and I guess that was how he liked it.' Smoke wreathed Otis's head, reluctant to move in the hot, airless morning.

'Heard he liked to gamble some,' Wes said.

'Reg'lar as clockwork.' Otis bobbed his

head. 'Once a month he and Milt Clayburn would take off for Laramie. Heard it was a real high stakes game.' He chuckled through the smoke cloud. 'You always knew when Frank lost. He sure hated losing.'

'Did he lose much?' Ben asked.

'I'll allow he came back happier more times than miserable. Another thing about Frank, and it became a sorta joke hereabouts, was the things he was going to do but never did.'

'How'd you mean?' Wes asked curiously.

'Member one time he reckoned to replace the corral fence. He got one side done and then lost interest. Never did finish the job. He was like that all the time. Had grand ideas and never the wit to finish 'em. Like that house of his, the one with the clay bricks and roof timbers like a cow's ribcage. He started that nigh on four year ago and everyone knew that he'd never finish it. Everyone, that is 'cept Frank. He wanted a house like he had seen back east one time, made of stone and not wood. Was gonna have a whole lot of these fancy bricks shipped out. Then he got to thinking. He figured he could save himself a whole heap of money if he made the bricks hisself, like the Mex's do. See the crick is clay bedded in parts. Got real excited over the idea.'

'You say that was four years ago?' Wes queried.

'T'ain't nothing wrong with your ears, young fella,' Otis commented dryly. 'Brought an old Mex in from Casper to show him how to make these 'ere clay bricks. Making the moulds, mixing the clay with sand and straw. Sun drying 'em real slow so they didn't crack.' Otis broke off for a chuckle and a puff of his pipe.

'Well that's real interesting, Otis, but...' Ben began.

'Ain't finished yet,' Otis barked, glaring at Ben. 'Like I was saying. He was all fired up at the time. Gonna build himself a real house. Helped him make the bricks mysel' on a coupla occasions. Then, like always, he lost interest. That was the kind of man

Frank Parsons was. Keen to start something, but never had the staying power to see it through. It came as no surprise to the folks in town.' Otis shook his head. 'Coulda had a real fine spread, but he was too mean with his money and too lazy in his ideas. "Hire and fire" Parsons they called him in town. Figure it was his meanness that drove his wife away. She upped stakes one day, took their boy and moved to Chicago. He never paid no mind. Seemed happier when she had gone.' Otis nodded. 'There was another time...' Otis ran on with a few more stories to outline the late Frank Parsons' meanness and failure to complete what he had started until Wes came to his feet and eased the stiffness from his buttocks.

'Well, I'll allow it's been nice talking to you, Otis, but we got some business in town.'

'I kin tell you plenty more,' Otis protested.

'Some other time, Otis,' Wes fended off. He could see the old man was lonely for someone to jaw to. He turned, after stepping from the veranda. 'Figure you to know the Boxed P as good as most. Any place around there where a careful man might want to hide something so that nobody else could find it?'

Otis frowned at Wes.

'Hell of a strange question, son?' he said guardedly.

'Isn't it just?' Wes agreed lightly and saw a crafty light appear in the old man's eyes.

'Reckon you've been listening to local gossip.'

'How's that?'

'There's those in town that reckon not all Frank's money went into the bank. Reckon he hid it somewhere on his land.' Otis gave a chuckle. 'Ol' Frank, he knew about the stories people were saying and it kinda tickled him. Reckon that's why he said what he did in the saloon, jus' afore he died.'

Both men turned and Wes felt his heart quicken.

'What was that?'

'You seem a nice coupla young fellas and

as you're a-helping Frank's kin, I'll tell you. Otis, he said to me, loud enough for half of Clancey's to hear, if'n you had my eyes you'd see the shine o' gold in mud and if'n I had yours I wouldn't.' He chuckled as the two eyed each other. 'Seen the expression you boys are wearing on other folks' faces that same night. Ol' Frank said later it'd give 'em somethin' to gossip about.' The rocker creaked.

'Did he mean anything by it?' Wes asked.

'D'yer mean, was he hinting at the hoard of money he was supposed to have buried at the Boxed P?' Otis's eyebrows knitted together. 'Can't rightly say. Mebbe it was all hogwash and Frank was just playing with folks. Mebbe they had him pegged right for a hoarder and he was just letting them know that he knew...?' Otis shrugged his thin shoulders. 'Frank was like that. He liked to string folks along, keep 'em guessing. If'n he did stash a poke and I'll allow he didn't, reckon his kin should find it. Good hunting boys. Let me know if'n you find anything.'

'Will do, Pop,' Wes promised.

On the journey back to the Boxed P they tossed various ideas back and forth over the meaning of Frank's cryptic words.

'Do you think it is a direct reference to the gold bullion?' Angela asked later as they discussed their visit to the chicken farmer.

'Reckon so, ma'am,' Ben said. The two sat in the parlour of the ranch house with Angela and Stumpy. It was hot and gloomy in the room, the curtains drawn in case any of Clayburn's men had the house under surveillance. They did not want Angela's presence known yet. It turned out to be a wise precaution for Stumpy said that he had seen two men go into a group of trees on a rise, half a mile south of the house. With the bunkhouse no longer there, the window could be seen from the rise.

'But what could it mean?' She eyed the two helplessly, sounds from Martha, in the kitchen, floating through to them.

'Ben here's of a mind it's been hidden in the creek. Sunk into the creek bed somewhere and covered with a layer of mud and shingle.'

'Wouldn't take a body long to dig out the creek bed, drop the gold in and let the creek bed settle on it,' Ben cut in.

'Yes, that could be it.' Angela's eyes lit up.

'I'll allow it's a good idea, 'cept the creek runs clear to the mountains. Where do you start looking?' Wes tossed back.

Angela's face fell.

'Do you think that's where he hid it, Wes?' She eyed Wes.

'Ain't sure, but I think Frank was a mite cleverer when it came to hiding the gold. If'n that was the case the whole creek bed could be searched in a coupla days, less if'n you had the men to hand. But first things first. We have gotta take care of those men in the trees. Can't let Clayburn have it all his own way.'

'We gonna shoot 'em, son?' Stumpy broke in, eyes sparkling with evil intent.

'Stumpy, you sure are a bloodthirsty old coot,' Wes reprimanded him lightly. 'You are gonna stay here. Ben an' I'll do the taking care part.'

The task of watching the house had fallen to Joe Santos and Smiley Jones. It was a chore both grumbled about when Billy Redland had hauled them out of bed at first light and explained their chore for the day. Smiley was still moaning as he sat with his back against a trunk.

'What the hell are we looking for anyway?' he groaned for the umpteenth time.

'Jesus, Smiley. We jus' report back on what Hardiman and Travis do all day. Don't you listen?'

Joe finished doing up his fly after relieving himself into a brush thicket.

'I know that, but why?'

'How the hell do I know? Keep an eye on the ranch is what we're told and report back all movements, 'specially the two strangers. Well that's what we do, so quit bellyaching.'

'Seen 'em ride out, seen 'em ride in. That sure is interesting,' Smiley said sourly.

'Don't know what you're beefing about,' Joe snapped back, setting his back against a tree bole, legs thrust out before him. 'This is better'n riding range in the hot sun. Me, I'm gonna make the most of it, sit here in the shade and enjoy the day.' Joe let out a contented sigh as he fished the makings from his pocket.

'Fun's over, boys. Best you don't make any sudden moves.' The quietly spoken words were accompanied by the ominous clicking of hammers being cocked. Both men froze. The undergrowth behind rustled. Making sure his hands were well away from his gun, Joe craned his head around and looked up into Wes's smiling face and Ben's hard, unsmiling countenance.

'Stand up, boys, and get rid of the hardware,' Ben ordered.

'We ain't doing anything, 'cept taking a rest,' Smiley said as he scrambled to his feet.

'Willy wasn't doing anything either,' Ben pointed out darkly.

'We had nothing to do with that. It was

Clayburn,' Smiley said quickly.

'The guns, real easy like,' Wes prompted and seconds later two pistols thumped to the ground.

'What'ya intend doing with us?' Joe asked uneasily.

'You're trespassing on Boxed P property. Could shoot you,' Wes said mildly. 'Could say you jumped us and there'll be no one around to say otherwise.'

Smiley's face whitened.

'Now hold on...'

'Move!' Ben said and minutes later the group stood at the rear of the trees where the two Clayburn riders had tethered their horses.

'You won't get away with killing us,' Joe said hoarsely, a sheen of sweat on his face. 'Not if'n you want to see the girl alive.'

'You won't be around to know one way or the other,' Wes pointed out idly. 'Now step outta them clothes of your'n.'

Smiley and Joe exchanged baffled glances. 'I don't know what you're up to, but...'

Smiley began.

'But nothing, boy,' Ben cut back. 'Your clothes, now!'

Under cover of two guns the two stripped to grubby long-johns.

'Ain't enough, gents,' Wes sang out. 'Everything. We want you mother-naked.'

'No way.' Joe backed, waving his hands before him. 'Ain't stripping nekid for no one.'

'Suit yourself,' Wes said and the Colt in his hand spoke twice and on the inside thighs of both Joe's legs, blood blossomed. Joe clasped himself and howled dancing in a circle. 'Ain't nothing but a couple of creases. Next time I'll be aiming a mite higher.'

Smiley was already stepping out of his long-johns and Joe followed suit, blood trickling down the insides of his legs, glaring hatefully at Wes.

'You best kill me now, mister. The next time I see you I'll be shooting,' Joe snarled.

'Look forward to it,' Wes replied evenly, unperturbed by the threat.

The two men were forced to mount their horses, facing the wrong way and then using sections of Joe's lariat, their hands tied behind their backs.

'Sure do make a real pretty sight don't they?' Wes sang out, a broad grin on his face as he stared at the two, red-faced men.

'You can't do this,' Smiley wailed.

'Maybe you want what happened to Willy?' Ben said. He drew his Colt and fired into the ground beneath the two horses. The animals bucked and whinnied before galloping off. Both men had to grab at their saddlehorns with their bound hands and grimly hold on.

'Try to stay in the saddle boys. It's a long walk,' Wes cried after them.

'I'll get you bastards for this!' Joe Santos raved back.

The two watched the naked riders vanish below a rise.

'That should smoke Clayburn's tail,' Wes said.

'You did what?' Angela could scarce

believe her ears as Wes recounted the outcome of their encounter with Smiley and Joe a little while later.

'Serve them no-accounts right,' Martha said.

'I'd sure liked to have seen that,' Stumpy chortled. 'By the time them boys get to the Circle C they'll have the sorest ar…!'

'Stumpy!' Ben and Wes shouted together causing the old man to draw to a halt, a guilty look flooding his face as he looked at Angela and Martha.

'Sorry, Miss Angie. Plumb forgot myself.'

Both Angela and Martha burst out laughing.

'I guess they will have,' Angela replied.

For Smiley and Joe their humiliation, when their horses carried them to the Circle C some two hours later, left them both scarlet faced. Cowboys gathered around unable to suppress grins and jeering catcalls. Milt Clayburn was livid when he saw the two. Their humiliation was his own.

'Get dressed,' he said thickly to the two

after they had been helped from the saddle and their bonds cut.

'We ain't letting 'em get away with this, boss, are we?' Billy Redland burst out indignantly.

Clayburn's cold eyes fixed on Billy.

'Round up some men and get my horse saddled. We'll pay the Boxed P a visit.'

'The boys'll appreciate that real fine,' Billy said, smiling vindictively, but Clayburn's next words wiped the smile from his face.

'There'll be no shooting on this trip. Hardiman and Travis need a little mental refreshing.'

'But, boss...' Billy began in protest.

'But nothing.' Clayburn's eyes settled on Billy.

'Make it quite clear that the first man to pull his gun will answer to me. They'll get their chance, but not today.'

Wes, cradling a Winchester in his arms, was at the gate when Clayburn and his men rode up. He had half expected a visit and put

Stumpy on watch. He had not been disappointed. Clayburn ordered his men to a halt and leaving them strung in a ragged line, proceeded on his own to face Wes. Clayburn's eyes flickered around before settling on the lone man.

'Where's your big friend?'

'Figure you'll find out if you and your boys are set on trouble,' Wes said mildly.

'You made a mistake doing what you did to Smiley and Joe. Time's running out for you and the girl. You can't afford to play games.'

'Maybe time's run out for you already, Clayburn,' Wes said enigmatically, his expression giving nothing away under Clayburn's startled scrutiny.

Clayburn's eyes narrowed.

'I don't know what game you're playing, Hardiman, but you're backed up against the wall with nowhere to go. I hold all the important cards, just remember that.' He turned his horse and looked back at Wes. 'Until tomorrow.'

ELEVEN

'You know where the gold is?' Five minutes later Angela treated Wes to an awed stare. In fact Wes was enjoying the mixture of expressions his sensational news had invoked.

'You've seen it?' Ben queried.

'We've all seen it without knowing what we were looking at. You see it just didn't sit right with me that Frank would do something as predictable as burying the gold. Too easy to spot freshly dug ground if'n you've a mind to look. No, Frank was a mite more clever. He never buried the gold at all.' Wes laughed at the ring of faces that showed increasing bafflement.

'How can it not be buried and we not see it? There are a few caves...'

'No caves, Miss Angie. It's not too many feet away from where we are standing now.

And how to see it yet not see it is quite simple. You make it into something different. Remember what Frank said to Otis? If you had my eyes you'd see the shine o' gold in mud and if I had yours I wouldn't. Well, I couldn't get that outta my mind. Then Clayburn said something just now that knocked all the pieces into place. He said my back was to the wall cause he was holding all the cards...'

'You sure can talk a lot when you've a mind to,' Ben cut in. 'How about telling us where it's at?'

Wes chuckled and raised his hands.

'OK, OK. The only place Frank could have hidden the gold in full view without it being seen was in the house he was building.'

'He built the house on top of it?' Stumpy asked.

'No, out of it. He incorporated the bars in the clay bricks he was making and built part of the house with them.'

A shocked silence followed his words.

Angela stared at him with the kind of hypnotic fascination only found between a snake and its prey.

'He built the house with gold bars?' she whispered huskily.

'Not quite,' Wes chuckled. 'The house he began four years ago. Everyone knew about it and his stop-and-start method of doing things. It was the perfect hiding place. No one would give a second thought to him building another part of it.' Wes shrugged.

'Well let's go and see if'n you're right,' Ben suggested.

'We'll need a sledge-hammer,' Wes voiced.

'I'll git one,' Stumpy volunteered.

They were all grouped before the half completed building when Stumpy arrived with the hammer. Wes had examined the structure, pulling the vine that overran it away until he found brickwork on one end wall that looked newer than the rest.

'How'd you feel about swinging a hammer, big fella?' he enquired of Ben and Ben grinned.

'Be my pleasure.'

'Right about here I should think.' Wes indicated a spot and moved to join the others as Ben swung the hammer.

The clay bricks flew apart as Ben demolished a section of the wall, then dropped the hammer, going to his knees before the pile of rubble. As the others closed in around him Ben wordlessly held up a gleaming, gold bar in his big hands.

'But how could he have done this without being seen?' Angela asked.

'Frank was a loner. Remember he only hired hands when he needed them. He was the only one here. The authorities spent the first couple of weeks searching further afield for the missing wagon, afore concentrating on the local area. Plenty of time for Frank to make his bricks. A few days to let them dry, then build the wall, sit back and let nature take over and cover it in creeper.' Wes smiled. 'We have the girl and we have the gold. Only one little problem left to clear up now.'

'Clayburn!' Ben said, scrambling to his feet.

'Any ideas?' Wes eyed Ben and Ben looked thoughtful.

'Seems his idea was to destroy the Boxed P,' Ben said slowly. 'He was responsible for Elroy catching a bullet and Willy's death and Stumpy here almost getting fried.'

'Not to mention the Bodines,' Wes tossed in casually, the mention of the name causing Angela to shudder.

'Best we show him how it should be done,' Ben ended quietly.

Wes studied his friend's grave face. The slow fuse that burned within had reached its limit and all hell was about to let loose. For an instant Wes almost felt sorry for Milt Clayburn, but the feeling passed quicker than the blink of an eye.

The morning shadows were shortening as the sun climbed higher and Billy Redland burst into Clayburn's study the following day. Clayburn's head snapped up in annoyance and he was ready to speak when Billy cried,

'He's here, boss, Hardiman, and coming in on a wagon.'

Clayburn came to his feet, words of reprimand forgotten as he buckled on a gunbelt before slipping on his jacket and hat.

'Are the men positioned?' he barked at Billy.

'Like you said, boss. Once he gets in the yard he'll be covered from all angles,' Billy smirked, but the smirk faded as he followed Clayburn from the room. 'There's only one of 'em. Hardiman.'

Clayburn came to a halt, frowning as he faced Billy.

'They're up to something. Keep your eyes open and warn the men to be on the lookout.'

Clayburn was on the porch as Wes brought the green flatbed to a halt in the centre of the devastation that had once been lawns and flowerbeds. A tarpaulin had been stretched over the low sides of the wagon to conceal whatever lay there. Clayburn's heart beat a little faster as he walked towards the wagon under Wes's neutral gaze. Was it possible that they had found the gold? Clayburn felt that this was a trick, a stall, but he could always hope.

'Where's your big friend?' He came to a halt before the wagon and stared suspiciously up at Wes.

At that precise moment Ben stood just within the trees behind and to one corner of the house. Since the discovery of the gold he had been busy. Yesterday afternoon he had gone into Freedom to purchase a few items for today's confrontation. The first of these lay on the arrow, and others like it, that he now notched to the bowstring. The bow, of springy juniper wood, and quiver of arrows were the trophies that had adorned the wall of the Boxed P ranch. The stick of dynamite attached to each arrow came from Freedom.

Ben had also bought a coil of slow-burning fuse and had experimented with various lengths until each stick had a ten-minute fuse. He eyed the roof of the house with its pyramids and four squat, wooden turrets at each corner and smiled thinly. From his hidden position looking down the side of the house, Ben observed Wes arrive and disappear around the front of the house. This was his signal to begin. He lit a small section of fuse to use as a lighter, touched it to the fuse of the loaded arrow and pulled back on the bowstring. He had practised with the added weight on the arrow and felt confident he could hit his targets. The first target would require the most accuracy. It was the turret on the far corner, overlooking the front of the house. If he missed the chances were that it would come down on top of Wes and the wagon. It was a grim thought that he shut out of his mind as he lined up on the target. The bowstring twanged musically as he discharged the arrow, with its destructive load, into the air and watched it arc upwards trailing a faintly smoking tail.

Ben held his breath, then released it in

relief as the flint head of the arrow thudded into the woodwork of the turret and held. The second arrow hit the rear turret with no problems and Ben moved on, keeping to the ring of trees.

Moving swiftly he sank a third arrow in the back wall just below the top, veranda roof. Seven minutes later the turrets at the other end of the roof had their deadly additions with a final one sunk half-way down the side wall. Losing the bow and remaining arrows in a convenient thorn bush, Ben slithered down a bank and circled the ranch to get back to a point on the trail where on the way in Wes had dropped him earlier. He had completed his part of the plan, now it was up to Wes to get himself out of there.

'Mighty fine day for a ride,' Wes amiably countered Clayburn's question, eyes on Billy and the four gunmen spread in a line behind Clayburn, remaining in position, their backs to the house as the man came forward.

'Don't play games with me, Hardiman.

Just now there are a dozen guns covering you. One signal from me and you are a dead man. Where's Travis?'

Wes answered the question by retrieving an object wrapped in cloth at his feet. He unwrapped it and tossed it contemptuously at Clayburn's feet.

'I thought you'd be a mite more interested in where the rest of that is.'

Clayburn stared down dumbstruck at the gold bar gleaming in the dust at his feet. Behind him Billy Redland was trying to see what had been thrown, wishing he'd gone closer with Clayburn.

'You've found it,' Clayburn whispered, sinking to his knees and cradling the gold bar in his trembling hands.

'Every one,' Wes agreed. He surreptitiously glanced towards his feet. A pocket watch lay on the boards. Ben had told him to start timing from the moment he passed through the gate. He estimated he now had one minute left.

Clayburn scrambled to his feet.

'You have it in the wagon?'

'Figured that would be a mite stupid of me in the circumstances,' Wes drawled lazily, but his insides were beginning to tighten in anticipation.

Clayburn eyed him oddly. 'The deal was the gold for the girl,' he said thickly.

'A million dollars for a girl. Could be a man'd be a fool to pay that kind of money.'

A tight smile spread across Clayburn's face. 'So you want the gold for yourself?'

'I'll take the deal you had with Frank,' Wes replied. The minute had passed and the second-hand was closing in on the second minute. A light sheen of sweat broke out on Wes's face and his heart began to hammer.

'How does your friend feel about this?'

Before Wes could answer an explosion ripped through the air. Clayburn craned his head around in time to see the corner turret explode into matchwood and take the roof corner with it in a roiling ball of smoke. The men nearest the house began to run for cover as fragments of wood began to rain down. Wes snapped the reins on the startled horse's back, yelling and dragging hard to the left. A second explosion demolished the rear turret and brought yelling, screaming servants tumbling from the house.

As the horse pulled the wagon in a tight circle, Wes leapt into the back and hunkered down low, still holding the reins. He straightened up the frightened animal and sent it charging forward.

From the windows of the long, bunk-house that faced towards the house, guns began to explode and bullets whine spitefully about Wes's head and thud into the low, wooden sides of the wagon. The idea was to get away in the resultant confusion, pick up Ben and draw Clayburn and his men into a more open, unprotected area. It could have worked, looked like it was going to work, but someone had the bright idea to aim for the horse and not the driver. A number of bullets smashed into the animal's body and head. The horse went down, lying heavily on the right shaft. Wes felt the wagon sliding away beneath him. He jumped clear as from behind the third arrow exploded leaving a gaping hole in the back wall of the house and destroying half of the top, rear veranda.

Wes hit the ground on his feet and went sprawling on to hands and knees, the rifle he had grabbed, flying from his grasp. Sharp stones bit into his knees and palms. The wagon ended up on its side, uppermost wheels spinning. Wes crawled behind it as lead pumped into the earth around him. Bullets were flying from all directions. Two of Clayburn's gunmen, who had been near the house, were charging towards the over-turned wagon, rifles firing from hip level. Wes swivelled about and snapped off two rapid shots from his Colt. His aiming was more accurate. Both gunmen folded, one with his forehead blown away.

Bullets thudded against the underside of the wagon. Wes crawled forward, using the dead horse's body for protection. Men had emerged from the bunkhouse and were advancing on the overturned wagon when Wes's bullets drove them to cover. One never made it. Wes caught a brief glimpse of Joe Santos diving for cover into the bunkhouse.

A fourth explosion rent the air. The once handsome ranch house now resembled an iced cake that someone had taken random bites from. Flames were beginning to leap from the roof and dark, angry smoke poured from the upper windows.

Wes got off two shots at a figure crouching with a rifle in the open doorway of the hayloft of the barn next to the bunkhouse. He was rewarded by the man throwing up his arms and tumbling out. A quick glance around showed Wes that Clayburn and Billy Redland had disappeared. He did not have time to contemplate their whereabouts. A hail of bullets drove him back into cover. He reloaded his Colt from his belt. Sweat ran down his face. There was blood on his left cheek from wood splinters thrown by impacting bullets.

The fifth and sixth explosions followed on each other's heels, tearing the side from the house and spilling the insides out. The entire upper section of the house was ablaze now, timbers cracking and exploding like miniature gunshots while a pall of black, angry smoke rose high into the air. Through bullet holes and cracks in the floor of the wagon Wes saw figures leaving the bunk-house, fanning out and hugging the ground. He stared about in desperation. There were trees at his back, but fifty yards of open ground to cover before reaching safety. He knew he would not last five yards out in the open.

'You're a dead man, Hardiman,' a voice called. Wes recognized it as belonging to Joe Santos.

'You're sure as hell trying,' Wes yelled back. 'And you ain't managed it yet.' A hail of bullets answered his brag, crashing against the exposed underside of the wagon, forcing him down on his face. So many bullets had hit the wood that they were now beginning to find their way through. He applied an eye to a crack and had to give Joe Santos grudging admiration. Four men were belly-down in the dust squirming towards him. Behind them another four crouched with rifles trained on the overturned wagon. If he tried to get a shot off he would expose himself to the waiting riflemen. He was trapped and time was running out fast.

A pistol cocking close to his ear froze him to the spot.

'Ain't it a pure shame you weren't looking over your shoulder?' Billy Redland stood over him, a wide grin on his face. 'You kin give up crawling in the dust, boys. Ol' Billy here's got him,' Billy crowed. He addressed Wes. 'I guess it's time to stand up and meet your Maker, son. Leave the gun where it's at.'

Wes came to his feet, the bitter taste of defeat sour in his mouth. He wondered what had happened to Ben? Maybe he had run into trouble too?

Smiley appeared at Billy's side, grinning wolfishly.

'Be a pure pleasure killing you, mister,' Smiley stated. 'If'n, of course, Mr Clayburn leaves enough of you alive.' He sniggered. Joe Santos had halted in the centre of the yard as the men formed a half circle about Wes and the overturned wagon. He wore a sour expression; he wanted Hardiman.

Milt Clayburn pushed his way through the men, still clutching the gold bar. Dirt and smuts from the raging fire streaked his face and there was a wild look in his eyes.

'Burn it, burn it all,' he hissed at Wes, pushing his face close to the others. 'I'll be able to build a bigger, better one.' He giggled, and ran a pink tongue over his lips regarding Wes balefully.

'With one little old gold bar?' Wes queried.

'You'll give the rest, I promise,' Clayburn said and the look in his eye chilled Wes.

An explosion shook the ground beneath their feet as the mid-section of the bunk-house disintegrated in a shuddering roar that had men cowering and wincing. Shod hooves rang on stone and pounded the dry earth and through a drifting cloud of smoke and dust Ben appeared. Astride one of Clayburn's horses, a roan he had found in a paddock, he rode without a saddle, one hand wrapped in the beast's mane. In the other hand his Adams spat lead as he charged the horse towards the stunned group. The dynamite stick he had tossed through a rear window of the bunkhouse had been his last.

Wes dived for his gun, rolling over on his back as a bullet from Ben's Adams tore into Billy's chest, spinning the man in a circle before slamming his face down in the dirt. Smiley fared no better. As Wes rolled on to his back he brought up his gun and fired. The .45 bullet destroyed Smiley's right eye before emerging through the top of his head in a gory splatter of blood, bone and brain.

Yelling, Ben charged the roan into the group of confused gunmen sending five of them down. Wes came to his feet, looking for Joe. A bullet from Joe's gun found him first, tearing into the muscle of his upper left arm. Cursing, Wes dived, rolled and came to his feet in a half crouch, left hand fanning in a blur as he pumped the hammer and fired four shots in rapid succession, each one tearing into the thin man's black clad body. Joe jerked like a marionette in the hands of a drunken puppeteer, eyes popping in surprise before they glazed. He was dead before he hit the ground. The surviving gunmen, seeing Billy and his crew downed, lost the will to fight and threw down their weapons, raising their hands.

Ben slid from the horse as Wes came across. Behind Ben the entire house was now engulfed in flame, wrapped in a blanket of glowing red that sent waves of heat flowing over them, even from this distance.

'What took you so long?' Wes asked with a crooked smile.

'Thought you could handle it on your own,' the big man parried. 'You OK?' He eyed Wes's bloodstained sleeve.

'Just a scratch. Where's Clayburn?'

Clayburn had retreated when the bunk-house had exploded and both men saw him moving across the front of the blazing house.

'It's over, Clayburn,' Wes yelled and was interrupted by the clatter of hooves a second time. Heads craned around to see Sheriff Caulder and a posse of men ride through the gates. Angela and Stumpy were with them. Caulder reined his horse to a halt, awe in his eyes as he looked at the flame-engulfed building.

'You boys don't do things by halves. Jeesus!' he breathed.

'It don't pay to get Ben here riled up,' Wes quipped. He pointed. 'Clayburn's making for the far corner of the house. Send some men to cut him off, Sheriff.'

'Didn't I tell you these boys were live 'uns?' Stumpy cackled proudly. 'Knowed it from the first time I clapped eyes on 'em. Yes sirree!'

While half of Caulder's men took off to intercept Clayburn, the other half rounded up the surrendered gunmen. Angela approached Wes, concern in her eyes at his wound, but he dismissed her attentions with a disarming smile.

'Ain't nothing, ma'am. Just a flesh wound. It can wait until Clayburn's caught.'

Riding in a wide circle the posse men drove Clayburn back across the front of the burning, timber blackened house. He was much closer to the fiery inferno than they and the heat for them was too much.

'The man's gonna fry if'n he stays there,' Caulder said. He raised his voice, cupping hands about his mouth. 'Give yourself up, Clayburn. Ain't no place to go now.' If Clayburn heard he gave no indication. He stood before the burning house, clutching the gold bar to his chest.

'He's too close,' Wes murmured. He pushed forward until the heat burnt and prickled his skin in blistering waves and still Clayburn was out of reach. 'Clayburn, come away,' he shouted hoarsely.

'It's mine, my gold,' Clayburn screamed,

stepping backwards, away from Wes, seemingly impervious to the blistering heat.

'The girl's safe, Clayburn.' Ben joined Wes. 'We got her away from the Bodines, so come away.'

Angela came forward, wincing at the heat.

'You're not going to take my gold away.' Clayburn continued to move backwards and Wes saw curls of dark smoke rising from the man's shoulders. His clothes were smouldering.

'You're too close, Clayburn,' Wes shouted desperately. 'Too close to the flames...' The words died in his throat, for at that moment Clayburn burst into flame, or rather his clothing did.

The hair vanished from his head in a flash of white, like a striking match. The stricken man turned and faced the crackling, spitting inferno for a second. The clothing was burnt from his back leaving boiling, blistered flesh. Angela screamed in sick revulsion and turned away. Wes drew her trembling body against his chest.

Clayburn turned jerkily away and Wes felt his stomach churn and tighten. Clayburn's eyes had boiled and exploded in their sockets, leaving gaping, black holes in flesh that was already peeling from the bone beneath. It seemed to Wes that flames were leaping from the man's gaping mouth, but that may have been imagination. The flaming structure was giving out thunderous cracks. Floors collapsing within the raging inferno filled the super-heated air with a hissing crash.

'I think she's collapsing,' Ben shouted.

The three turned and ran as the charred, burnt thing that had once been human sank to its knees, the gold bar bright in its flesh melted hands. With a roar that sounded like a dozen waterfalls uniting the flaming structure collapsed and buried the pitiful remains of Clayburn beneath a thick ridge of glowing embers and black, charcoaled spars.

Wes turned and stared, felt pity for the man who lay beneath it and shook his head.

Gold had driven the man to murderous lengths and his own untimely, shocking end.

'Let's get out of here,' Wes said thickly.

The following morning Wes and Ben watched the last of the gold bars loaded into a wagon for its journey to the jail in Freedom: the only place strong enough to hold it while awaiting collecting by the army in a few days.

'What will you do now?' Angela asked the two. Wes had his arm in a sling while his wound, a deep gouge across the muscle, mended. The two had said their goodbyes to Martha and Stumpy and now stood by their horses.

'Head for Tucson and pick up another assignment,' Wes said.

'It'll be a mite quiet here without you two around,' she remarked with a smile. 'What about the money I owe you for my marker? How do I pay you back?'

Wes grinned as he pulled the said document from a pocket and handed it to her.

'You more'n paid it back with the return of the gold bullion.' He swung awkwardly into the saddle and looked down at her. 'You've got what it takes to be a rancher ma'am and don't let anyone tell you otherwise.'

At the bar of the Red Dog saloon in Tucson, three weeks later, the big stranger shouldered Wes roughly aside as he shouted for the barkeep.

'That wasn't very friendly, stranger,' Wes pointed out.

'Wanna do somethin' about it?' the stranger asked nastily.

'Wouldn't be too sensible of me would it?' Wes said, eyeing the man up and down as an expectant hush settled over the room.

'Sure wouldn't,' the stranger agreed with a smirk, feeling he had the situation under control.

'Gotta dollar that says I've got more sense than you,' Wes said, drawing the dollar from his pocket.

The publishers hope that this book has given you enjoyable reading. Large Print Books are especially designed to be as easy to see and hold as possible. If you wish a complete list of our books please ask at your local library or write directly to:

Dales Large Print Books
Magna House, Long Preston,
Skipton, North Yorkshire.
BD23 4ND

Wl
of
loc
Be
the
it.
wa
Pa
Bc
sh
de
an
Ha
th